Fighting Tackle

Fighting Tackle

by Matt Christopher

Illustrated by Karin Lidbeck

Little, Brown and Company
Boston New York Toronto London

Text copyright © 1995 by Matthew F. Christopher
Illustrations copyright © 1995 by Karin Lidbeck

First Paperback Edition

Library of Congress Cataloging-in-Publication Data
Christopher, Matt.
Fighting tackle / by Matt Christopher ; illustrated by Karen Lidbeck. — 1st ed.
    p.   cm.
    Summary: When he becomes stronger but slower, Terry must deal with
being moved from defensive safety to offensive tackle on his
football team and with the fact that his younger brother, who was
born with Down's Syndrome, is becoming a faster runner.
    ISBN 0-316-14010-4 (hc)
    ISBN 0-316-13794-4 (pb)
    [1. Football — Fiction.   2. Brother — Fiction.   3. Down's Syndrome —
Fiction.   4. Mentally handicapped—Fiction.]   I. Title.
PZ7.C458Fi   1995
[Fic] — dc20   94-19680

10 9 8 7 6 5 4 3 2 1

MV-NY

Published simultaneously in Canada
by Little, Brown & Company (Canada) Limited

Printed in the United States of America

To Brenda, Tom, Robbie, and Jessica

Fighting Tackle

1

Terry McFee looked down the length of the gridiron toward the opposing team's offense all lined up and ready for the play.

They were so far, he could hardly make out the individual players. They were all dressed in black. Black helmets. Black jerseys. Black pants. They formed an enormous black wall.

The quarterback barked out the signals. As the center snapped the ball, the split end took off down the field. The quarterback skipped back and threw. Hard. The ball soared high into the air.

Terry ran as fast as he could, trying to anticipate where the offense and the ball might meet. With luck, he would be able to intercept the pass before the receiver knew what happened.

But suddenly his pace grew slower. He churned his legs with all his might, but he couldn't make any headway. The black wall moved steadily toward him — and the split end farther away.

Hup! Hup! Hup!

Who was calling signals in the middle of a play? And why weren't his teammates blocking the black team's offense?

Hep! Hep! Hep!

Everything seemed to be going in slow motion. Terry pushed his body forward. He'd just spotted the split end when out of nowhere a gigantic football came flying through the air, heading right toward his man. But if Terry could get there first, he could block the pass — or better yet, catch it!

Hick! Hick! Hick!

A black-uniformed figure loomed large in front of him, long arms waving. To his horror, Terry saw suction cups where the receiver's hands should have been. But the ball was coming straight at him, so he thrust his emotions aside, flexed his knees, and sprang high into the air, arms outstretched.

But the mutant split end jumped higher — and caught the ball. He stumbled over the sidelines, completing the pass but ending the play.

2

Tick! Tick! Tick! *Riiing! Briiinng!*

Instead of a whistle, a bell was ringing in the distance.

Terry looked toward the stands where the sound was coming from.

They were completely deserted — except for one person. Right in the middle, he saw his little brother, Nicky. At the sound of the bell, Nicky came running down from the stands and onto the field. Staring his brother right in the eye, Nicky started shaking him and crying out his name. The bell kept ringing and ringing and ringing.

"Terry! Come on, get up, you'll be late for school!"

The bell stopped. Terry opened his eyes and looked up from his bed. Nicky was standing there in his blue and white striped pajamas and holding the alarm clock.

"What's the matter, Terry? Didn't you hear it go off?" Nicky asked, rubbing his eyes.

Terry groaned. Then he smiled at Nicky and hopped out of bed.

Nicky was a little chunky from his shoulders to

3

his hips. He had long, spindly legs that seemed like they belonged to someone else. The only other thing about him that stood out was his face. It still had a babyish look to it, and his eyes were sort of small for a kid his age.

Terry knew that these features showed that Nicky had Down's syndrome. It was something that Nicky was born with and set him apart in some ways from kids his age. But Terry was so used to his kid brother, he hardly noticed any difference.

Others did, though. Every once in a while, Terry saw someone snicker or whisper behind Nicky's back when he was a little slow or awkward. They thought that Down's syndrome made Nicky some kind of weirdo.

It made Terry so mad, he wanted to belt whoever it was. But his parents had taught him a long time ago that that wouldn't change anyone's mind. He had to be patient, and whenever he got a chance, he had to explain that Down's syndrome wasn't anything bad — and it didn't make Nicky any worse than anyone else. It simply meant that he learned different things at his own speed. He might stop learning at some point, but he might go on forever. Nicky could become an astronaut, for all anyone knew!

Terry watched Nicky pad back to his own bedroom. He was relieved to be awake and realize that it had only been a dream. There was no "black team"! He hadn't missed blocking an important pass just now after all.

And then he remembered the game with the Skyhawks two days before. He sat back down on the bed, reliving that awful moment.

Terry's team, the Clippers, were ahead, 17–13. The Skyhawks had the ball on their own forty-yard line. It was first down and ten to go with less than a minute and a half left in the game.

"No mistakes!" shouted Coach Butterfield to his Clippers defensemen. "Hold 'em back there!"

The fans filling the stands were on their feet, cheering on their respective teams. The cheerleaders were screaming at the top of their lungs. The noise was deafening, but exhilarating. Terry's heart raced with excitement as he lined up in the backfield. As the team's free safety, he'd been running hard almost the whole game, but he didn't feel tired. The Clippers were only a minute and a half away from winning the season's opening game!

Freddy Wilkins, the Skyhawks' quarterback, called out his signals.

"Hut! Hut! Hut!"

Everyone expected the long bomb. Freddy had a great arm, even though he hadn't connected all that well with his receivers during this game. They were held pretty much in check by a heads-up Clippers secondary defense.

Terry could smell the tension in the air. It had the odor of trampled grass, mud, dirt, and sweat all rolled into one.

"Hike!" Freddy grabbed the ball and skipped back a few feet. He faked a handoff to Louie Larue, then pushed him into the slot to the left of center. Planting his feet securely, Freddy drew back and sent the ball way downfield toward his split end, Moe Thompson, a nimble, long-limbed boy who looked like he should be playing basketball. He was the Skyhawks' number one receiver.

Not this time, though, Terry thought, spinning around. I can get there. I can block that pass. I've outrun him most of the time this game. Just one more.

He was a good five yards away when he saw Moe's outstretched palms gather in the pigskin. Moe was off like a shot.

Terry used the last of his strength to go after him, but he didn't have a prayer. Moe had a clear field all the way down to the goal line. He practically walked into the end zone. The Skyhawks took the lead, 19–17, and stretched it 20–17 with a successful extra-point kick.

The Clippers tried hard when they got possession of the ball. But it was no use. In the time remaining, they couldn't even get close enough for a decent field-goal attempt. The final score told the story: Skyhawks 20, Clippers 17.

"TERREEE!"

Nicky's voice cut into Terry's thoughts. He shook his head to erase the memory of the scoreboard. As Coach Butterfield had told them in the locker

room, it was just the first game of the season. If they really dug in during this week's practices, their next game could end differently.

With a determined nod of his head, Terry stood up and started to get dressed. He couldn't wait for his chance to show the coach he was ready to go that extra mile.

He got his chance the very next practice session. Coach Butterfield worked the defense team hard. Terry played nonstop for what seemed like hours. But he loved every minute of it.

Throughout the practice, he could hear Nicky yelling enthusiastically for him from the stands. He was able to block it out most of the time, but once Nicky's voice cut through his concentration.

Danny Stowe, the Clippers' quarterback, had just thrown a high spiral. It was probably heading out of bounds, but Dirk Solomon, the wide receiver, had a way of leaping up for a grab right at the sidelines. Terry couldn't take that chance. Solomon was his man.

The Clippers' ace receiver was a good ten yards

away from him. Terry turned on the juice. He reached Dirk just as the ball began to arc downward. But as he prepared to jump for the ball, Nicky yelled.

"TERREEEE!"

Terry faltered just for a second. That was all Dirk needed. He leaped into the air and grabbed the ball just before he skipped across the white sideline marker. What could have been an interception wound up being a completed pass.

Darn that Nicky! thought Terry. I bet I would have had it if he hadn't yelled!

Then he shook his head. Nicky's enthusiastic shouts had helped him find hidden strength more times than he could count. Who knows? he thought. Maybe I wouldn't be as good without my own personal cheering squad!

The coach's whistle blew to call both offensive and defensive teams back over to the bench.

Terry chugged back, breathing heavily as he approached the water jug. He took a deep, long drink, then flopped down on the bench. When he took off his helmet, his brown hair stuck to his forehead like little spikes.

"Okay, guys, settle down for a minute," said Coach Butterfield. "You've been working hard out there, so relax for a minute. Right, time's up!"

The guys all laughed. The coach was really serious about the game, but he had a sense of humor, too. Everyone on the team liked and respected him.

"Most of you look good out there," the coach went on. "Offense, you're moving the ball in the air just like you should be. But we need more power to open up those holes for the runners. Defense, you're a little slow reading the plays. But you're getting good coverage for the most part. Still, I know we can do better. So I'm going to try a few changes. We'll just see how these work out."

Terry slumped over and let the tension in his body settle down. The coach had done this before, but it didn't mean much to him. He was fast on his feet, a natural safety. It was the position he'd played from the start, and he'd always done a good job.

"Marsh, I want you to go in at right guard, and Russ Millick, let's see what you can do at fullback. Now, on defense, I want to see McFee at nose tackle. . . ."

Terry blinked in surprise. What? There had to be some mistake, he thought. I'm not big enough for the line. Besides, I'm too fast. They need me as a safety. I block more passes —.

"That's it," the coach concluded. "So let's give it a try. We'll spot the ball at midfield and run a few easy plays. No really hard contact. Danny," he called to his quarterback, "I want you to keep it on the ground for now. We'll try some pass plays later."

As the guys started to run out onto the field, Terry went over to the coach.

"Are you sure you want me in the line?" he asked. "I mean, I . . . I never played that position. I don't think . . . I mean . . . I don't know the plays."

"Just go out there and do what any defensive lineman should," said Coach Butterfield. "Go after the man with the ball. And leave the coaching to me."

Terry jogged out onto the field. He was so surprised by the switch that when they lined up across from the offense, a few of the guys practically had to push him into his slot as the nose tackle.

Across from him and a few yards back, he could hear Danny Stowe calling out the numbers: "Six! One! Seven! Hike!"

He recognized the signals for a handoff. His years of playing safety told him to relax a little. He wouldn't have to race with a receiver.

But that momentary letup was enough for the center, Mike Randall. Terry felt Mike's hulking form come crashing into him. An instant later, he was flat on his back. A scurry of feet next to his prostrate form told him that someone was making tracks downfield.

A whistle blew and he got up. Tony Glover, the substitute free safety, had brought down the runner some twenty yards from scrimmage.

"Sorry about that," Mike called over. "Didn't mean to hit you that hard."

Terry waved at him to show that he was okay. Then he turned and jogged down to join the lineup at the goal line.

13

"Heads up, guys!" shouted the coach from the sideline.

"TER-REEEEE!"

". . . Seven! Hike!"

Confused by all the shouting, Terry didn't hear Danny call the whole play. Once more, he missed his moment — and his block. Terry found himself down on the ground again as Danny carried the ball by him in a classic "quarterback sneak."

Three short blasts on the whistle got the whole team's attention.

"Okay, let's call it a day," said the coach, coming out to the middle of the field. "But first, don't move. Just sit down where you are — and take a look around."

Great, thought Terry. I don't even have to get up. I'm already down.

Coach Butterfield smiled as he looked around. "I swapped you around for a number of reasons. One is to show you that every position is important, not just yours. You'll play better as a team if you remember that. Another reason was to get a sense of how some of you might do in another position. Oh,

I know, you don't know the plays that well and you haven't trained for the backfield or the line or whatever. But we'll start working on that one by one at our next practice. Meanwhile, let's see five laps before you hit the showers."

"TER-REEEEE!"

Terry heard one of his teammates snicker.

For crying out loud, there he goes again, thought Terry. I'm going to have to talk to Nicky when I get home. He might be distracting some of the other players, too. But right now, I'm going to show the coach what he's missing if he really takes me out of the safety slot. Watch my dust!

He joined a few other linemen and hit the dirt track that surrounded the field. His first burst of speed put him in front of the pack. But that didn't last. The long hours on the field had taken their toll. One by one, some of the others passed him. His pads and helmet suddenly felt very heavy as he trudged along in the middle of the group of runners.

This wasn't a race. There was no ribbon to cross at the end. But Terry had always tried to do his best on laps. Now his legs were letting him down a little. He'd finish the five laps — but certainly not ahead of most of the guys.

As he counted off the fifth and final approach to the starting point, he was really glad that practice had ended for that day.

When he was leaving the field, Terry saw Coach Butterfield talking to Evan Marsh. He could hear the coach saying, "I know you can catch the ball, Evan. But I think you'll be more help to the team in the guard's slot. You're strong, real strong, and we need strength in the offensive line."

"But coach, I—"

"Evan, trust me," said Coach Butterfield. "You want to do what's right for the team, don't you?"

"Uh-huh," Evan said, nodding.

"Okay, then, hit the showers for now. We'll work on those plays from the guard's position at our next practice."

The coach gave Evan a playful tap on the shoulder as the new offensive lineman left the field.

"Something on your mind, Terry?" Coach Butterfield asked as Terry approached.

"I . . . uh . . . well, I heard you talking to Evan, coach," said Terry. "And I . . . uh . . . well, I was wondering why you don't want me to play safety anymore. I mean, for the good of the team I think I'd be better off there. Or didn't I do a good job at safety?"

"Of course you did, Terry," said the coach, quietly. "But you can make a contribution to the team in any number of positions. I'm just trying to find the best spot for you — and for the team. You're in excellent physical condition. But you're getting bigger. The way your upper body is filling out, we can't expect you to be as light on your feet as you have been at safety. So let's see how well you can play in the line. I think you have the makings of a fine nose tackle."

"Sure, coach, sure," murmured Terry. "I'll go get cleaned up now."

"Say, Terry," the coach asked, "wasn't that your kid brother, Nicky, I heard in the stands?"

Terry reddened.

"Yes, it is. I—"

"Heck of a pair of lungs on that boy," said the

17

coach, smiling. "You might ask him to keep his enthusiasm in check during practices, but make sure he's at all our games. We need someone like that cheering for the Clippers!"

Terry breathed a sigh of relief.

2

After he had showered and dressed, Terry left the locker room for the fifteen-minute walk home. As usual, Nicky was waiting right outside the door.

"Terry! Terry!" he shouted, even though his big brother was only a few feet away. "Dad's here!" It seemed like everything was a big deal to Nicky, Terry thought.

Right now, Nicky was pleased as a parsnip that he knew before Terry that Mr. McFee was going to drive them home.

It didn't happen that often. Mr. McFee's job as a construction supervisor didn't give him a lot of afternoons when he could come home early.

"So, how's the star safety?" he asked as the boys climbed into the front seat of his pickup truck. "How many passes did you ruin for poor Danny and Dirk?"

19

Nicky fumbled with the buckle of his seat belt as Terry clicked the catch on his.

"Not a lot," said the older boy, reaching over to wiggle the tip of Nicky's belt into the slot. "I didn't get that much of a chance."

"Coach tell Danny to keep the ball on the ground?" asked Mr. McFee, guiding the truck neatly between the two stone pillars that marked the entrance to the school grounds.

"Terry's in the line, Dad!" Nicky blurted out before Terry got around to telling his father. "He doesn't chase the ball. He chases the one throwing the ball, you know, the what's the name?"

"The quarterback," said Terry.

"The quarterback," Nicky repeated softly.

"Right, I go after whoever has the ball. Coach is trying different kids in different spots," Terry explained. "Doesn't mean anything. I could end up playing anywhere. I could even go over to the offense and be a receiver."

"You could be a receiver?" asked Nicky.

"Sure, why not? I covered enough receivers to know their patterns," said Terry.

"Hmmmm, not quite the same as being able to catch the ball," said Mr. McFee. "Not that I don't think you can do anything you set your mind to—"

"Me, too?" asked Nicky.

"You, too," his father replied. "It's just that you're such a natural on defense, Terry. You pick up on the keys right away. I mean, you always seem to figure out real fast what the play is going to be — and then move on it. I don't think the coach is going to want to lose that."

"Maybe," mumbled Terry. "Hey, Dad, can we stop for an ice cream?"

"And ruin your dinner? Your mother won't like it, but—"

"Please, Dad, please!" Nicky whined.

"Okay, but you'd better finish your dinner, both of you. Even the part you don't like."

"Don't worry, Dad," Terry said. "I can't think of anything I don't like to eat lately. It's like I'm always hungry."

"Well, you're definitely filling out, son," said Mr. McFee. "When I was your age, I ate everything in sight. Your grandmother used to say I grew an inch

21

a night. But it looks to me like you're getting broader, Terry, not taller. I think you must take after your mother's side of the family. You're starting to look a bit like Uncle Dan!"

Uncle Dan was shaped like a bulldog — short, stocky legs and broad, strong shoulders. He was one of Terry's and Nicky's favorite relatives. A good athlete in his younger years, Uncle Dan could lift more weight than Terry and his father combined. But when it came to running, Terry was the clear winner, with Nicky usually coming in a close second.

Terry grinned. If there was one thing Nicky loved more than watching him play football, it was running. He glanced over at his younger brother. Nicky was busy watching a dog lap up a bit of spilled ice cream.

Then Mr. McFee returned with their cones, and Terry turned his attention to more important matters.

"More rice pudding?"

"No, believe it or not, I'm full," Terry replied to his mother's question. "I think I'd better not."

"That makes Nicky the champ. He's had 'thirds.' You're always hungry these days," Mrs. McFee said, smiling at her younger son. "I wonder if you'll be able to make it around the track tomorrow morning."

"I will, Mom! I will!" Nicky insisted.

"Maybe both of you boys should go for a run when the sun comes up," said Mr. McFee. "You look like a few early morning laps wouldn't be such a bad idea, Terry."

"What do you mean?" But even as he asked the question, Terry knew what his father meant. All during dinner he'd been trying to figure out why Coach Butterfield had switched him to the line.

"It's just that running is sometimes a good way to clear your mind," said Mr. McFee. "You've been somewhere off in the distance since I picked you up after practice today. Maybe a good, hard run will help you figure out whatever's bothering you."

Terry nodded. "You're right, Dad," he said. "I guess I'm still a little upset about the coach putting me in at tackle. I just don't feel right there. Maybe a good run will help."

"I'll race you," Nicky offered.

"No, thanks," said Terry, laughing. "I don't know whether being beaten by my kid brother is what I want right now."

Nicky's love of running was an ongoing joke in the McFee family. Both boys were fast, but Nicky somehow managed to put on a burst of speed in the short distances that made him tough to beat. Terry always thought Nicky would make a good sprinter if only he had the proper coaching. In fact, he had once suggested that Nicky might have fun practicing with the middle school's track team.

But Nicky had balked at the idea. Both Terry and Nicky shared the same sunny dispositions and willingness to give 100 percent, according to their mother. But Terry knew that Nicky sometimes had a hard time learning new things. He needed to get used to an idea gradually before he would accept it.

Deep down Terry also knew that there was a chance that Nicky's ability to learn would always be frustratingly slow. Still that didn't mean Nicky couldn't succeed at whatever he set his mind to. Take running, for example. His kid brother *could* keep getting better at running if he practiced hard at it every day.

So Terry hadn't given up. For the past few weeks, every time he and Nicky ran together on the school's dirt track, Terry brought up the fact that this was the same place the track team practiced. He was careful to explain the different track events and to describe a typical practice. He had even introduced Nicky to the track coach. And it seemed his perseverance was paying off. Every time the word "running" came up lately, Nicky took it to mean "race."

Terry grinned at his little brother.

"You know what, champ?" he said. "I'll make a deal with you. We'll race tomorrow morning. The winner gets to pick the Saturday night video. Okay?"

"Okay!" shouted Nicky.

3

The early fall sun had barely risen when the two boys reached the schoolyard. As they passed between the stone pillars, Terry could see a thin layer of mist rising from the dark black oval that wound its way around the football field.

"How many laps?" asked Terry.

"Ten!" said Nicky, giggling.

"Don't be nuts," said Terry. "We'll do two. That way you'll have a chance."

"Oh, yeah?" said Nicky.

"Oh, yeah!" Terry said firmly.

By now they had reached the fifty-yard marker on the side of the field. This was where they always began their races.

As usual, Terry took the place of the announcer.

"And now, ladies and gentlemen, the big race between the defending champion, Nicky McFee,

26

and his older but wiser big brother, the dynamic free safety . . ."

His voice broke. Quickly, he recovered and went on.

". . . now playing a variety of positions for the Clippers, Terry McFee. Racers, take your positions! Ready! Set!"

He paused for Nicky to give the final signal.

"Go!" shouted the younger McFee.

They took off counterclockwise down the track. Nicky bolted out to an early lead before settling down to a steady pace. Terry kept an eye on him and adjusted his own run to the same level of speed. Around the first turn they went and then into the backstretch, like a pair of frisky colts in the dewy morning air.

As they reached the second turn and headed for the homestretch, Nicky was still a few paces ahead. Terry knew that he could put on some speed and beat him at the wire, but he wouldn't do that. Winning at running means a lot to that guy, he thought. Still, I have to make it look convincing.

He broke from his steady lope and bore down.

That was when he noticed something different. Instead of the seamless shift in gears he usually felt when he put on the speed, he found it was taking an extra effort to move faster. Of course, he could outrun his kid brother. If he really wanted to, he could leave him in the dust. But he had to work just a little harder to do that.

Thinking about all this slowed Terry down a lot. Nicky pulled way ahead and crossed the imaginary finish line well in front of him.

By the time Terry got there, Nicky was jumping up and down.

"I won! I won! I get to pick the Saturday night movie!" Nicky shouted.

Terry nodded. "Right," he said. "You're still the champ."

In the distance, the two boys heard the sound of a motor vehicle. Mr. McFee's pickup truck pulled up at the far end of the field.

"Anyone want a lift home to get ready for school?" he called over to them.

"Sure!" Nicky called back. He turned to Terry,

slapped him on the arm, and cried, "Tag! You're it!" and raced off toward the truck.

Terry just shook his head and trotted off after him.

He's ready, he thought. Time for Plan B of "Operation Nicky." Out loud, he said, "Hey Dad, can I talk to you after breakfast?"

At school that day Terry got a pass to visit the track coach. As he'd hoped, Ms. Phillips was as enthusiastic about his idea as his parents had been.

"If you think your brother would be comfortable practicing with the track team, I see no reason why he shouldn't be given the chance. They'll be using the outside track, the one you and Nicky run on now, until the weather gets chilly. When they move inside, he'll probably be enjoying himself so much that it will be easy for him to adjust to the change," she said.

She reached into her desk and pulled out her calendar. "And here's something else you might want to think about — the Special Olympics. You've heard about them?"

30

Terry shook his head.

"Basically, the Special Olympics offer physically and mentally handicapped athletes a chance to participate in athletic events similar to those of the regular Olympics. However, these games stress building the individual's self-esteem over competition. For example, every participant gets an award of some sort, not just those who win first, second, and third. The official games don't happen until the summer, but I believe there are certain ongoing sessions throughout the year that Nicky might have fun taking part in once he's at ease running with people other than you. I'll send some booklets to your home for you and your parents to look over."

Terry thanked her and headed to study hall.

Well, he thought, I've done all I can. Now it's up to Nicky.

That afternoon, right after school ended, the coach had scheduled the first practice before the Clippers' next game. They were scheduled to play the Cougars on Saturday afternoon, and he had five days to get the team in shape. Terry put all

31

thoughts of Nicky out of his head and concentrated on practice.

Coach Butterfield told Mike Randall, the center, to call out the numbers for the warm-up drills the team did every day. Terry lined up as usual with the defense and skipped his way through obstacles, threw blocks at the tackling dummy, and butted up against whoever lined up opposite him.

Ray Shale, the left tackle for the Clippers' offense, was a little slow slamming back at him and ended up on his back.

"Whew! You're getting real tough, Terry," said Ray, rubbing his bottom as he got up. "You'll do great as a tackle."

Terry nodded. Even though he wanted to give the team his best, he wasn't so sure that was where he wanted to play. Seemed to him that all linemen did was bang up against the other guys. Once in a while, if they were lucky, they broke through and got a piece of the runner. If they were extra lucky, they might even get to bring down the opposing quarterback. But most of the time, when he watched the college teams or the pros on TV, it looked like pretty dull work being a grunt in the defensive line.

These thoughts slam-banged around Terry's mind as the warm-up ended. The coach blew his whistle and called them all over to the bench.

"Okay, here's the way I want to see you line up for the first scrimmage this afternoon. Offense!"

He ran down the list of offensive players he'd been putting together the past few weeks. There were no surprises. Danny Stowe would be the quarterback on any team. He was tall for his age, but strong and wiry. His long arms seemed to stretch over the pack when he got set to pass. With enough time, he usually hit his mark. That was generally Dirk Solomon, the split end. But Danny was sharp-eyed. He could pick out an open receiver in a split second if necessary.

"Defense! Okay, at left corner, I want Huey Page. Left end, let's see Sid Keller. At nose tackle, Terry McFee. John Crum, I want you . . ."

Tackle! There it was. The coach isn't even going to let me start out in the safety spot, Terry thought, and groaned to himself.

". . . and in the free safety spot, let's see Tony Glover."

Tony! I can run rings around him! Terry thought.

Coach Butterfield continued, "Danny, you run some pass patterns with the offense. I'm going to work with the defense. First the linemen. Okay, let's have Keller, McFee, and Crum up here for starters. The rest of you, gather 'round and listen."

Terry ambled over to where the coach stood. He looked around at a bunch of chunky, hefty kids beefed up by a lot of padding and protective gear.

"Okay, what's the first thing all good defensemen have to know?" Coach Butterfield asked.

"How to bring down the guy with the ball?" Sid Keller suggested.

"That's not the first thing," said the coach patiently.

"How to make your block?" asked John Crum.

"Part of it, but not the very first thing," said the coach. "We're going to get right down to the beginning — and that is, your stance. Okay? Now, we start with the three-point stance, with your weight a little bit forward. It's important that you're low to the ground, too, for balance. You're going to have to move fast, and that's usually going to be straight ahead."

Boy, this really is getting down to basics, Terry thought. But he figured the coach knew what he was doing. For the next half hour, along with the other linemen he worked on all the fundamentals — with a special emphasis for him on what the defensive tackle's job would be.

There was something about a good workout that revved him up. Even though he wasn't chasing runners from the backfield, Terry had to put a lot of effort into keeping up with the coach's instructions.

"Good move, Terry, you're starting to get it," said the coach after Terry had just made a solid block. "You're going to do fine. Now, secondary, get over here. You guys have a lot to learn before the game on Saturday. Tony, you're going to have to learn how to read plays from the safety's position. Terry can go over some of them with you later on. Right now, let's work on the basics."

So now he was supposed to help someone else take over his position, the one he really wanted to play? Terry wasn't so sure he wanted to do that.

He took off his helmet and walked over to the bench. He wondered whether he should just keep walking straight off the field and into the locker room.

But that didn't make sense. He loved football. Being able to play with the Clippers was a dream come true. What difference did it make which position he played as long as he helped out the team, right?

In his mind, he ran through all the pro and college players he admired. Look at how many of them had switched around positions when they were starting out. Johnny Unitas wasn't always a quarterback. Bob Gladieux had been a running back at Notre Dame before he ended up as a nose tackle for the Patriots and Redskins. The Football Hall of Fame probably had a whole gallery of famous switches in position.

No, he had to stick with it and do whatever the coach said. There was no knowing how it would turn out.

He put his helmet back on and called over to Sid

Keller, "Hey, want to show me how you work that shoulder and forearm charge?"

Might as well learn to do it right, he thought. As long as I'm playing defensive tackle, I'm going to be a good one.

4

Terry! Terry! Guess what?" Nicky called over to him as he left the locker room after practice.

"Guess why I wasn't at your football practice today!" the younger boy cried out. "I'm going to run with the track team every day after practice, that's why! Mom and Dad and the coach said I could. I'll have a uniform just like the real team members, too, even though I won't be on the team. I get to start on Friday."

"Really?" Terry feigned surprise. "Nicky, that's great! You'll show those guys what a *real* runner can do. I'm proud of you, little brother."

Nicky grinned happily.

"So what events are you thinking about trying?" Terry asked.

Nicky looked puzzled. "Running," he said. "Like I do with you."

"Sure, but there're all kinds of running, remember?" Terry said. He suddenly realized that Nicky could very well be confused his first practice, even though he had tried to clue him in to what typically went on. "Tell you what — on our way home we'll stop by the library and pick up a book on track. I remember looking at one with a lot of great pictures in it when I was your age."

"You wanted to go out for track?" asked Nicky.

"Not really," said Terry. "I always wanted to play football. But I'd been winning races since I was in kindergarten, you know, fastest kid in the class. So I thought I ought to check out track. But I ended up sticking with football."

"But I don't want to play football," said Nicky. "I can't do all those plays and things. Maybe I shouldn't do anything."

"No way!" said Terry. "You're a terrific runner. You'll have fun with the track team. Just listen carefully to the coach and do the best you can."

"Like you? Like you playing in the line now?" asked Nicky.

"Just like that," said Terry. He caught his breath.

39

He remembered how he'd felt like chucking it all in just a little while ago.

And wouldn't *that* have been a good example to Nicky, he thought.

During the next few days, Terry did his best to learn all he had to about the nose tackle's spot. And in his off moments, he worked with Tony Glover. To tell the truth, that wasn't a lot of fun. Tony seemed to be learning faster than he himself was. But the coach didn't let up on either of them.

"Okay, Terry, you have to key in on the offense just as much from the line as you did from the back wall," the coach said. "For instance, if the guard over you pulls back behind the center, you have to figure it's the trap — and make your move. Let's give it a try."

He blew the whistle.

"Danny, come on over here. Listen, I want you to run these three plays," said Coach Butterfield. He turned away so that no one could see what he was saying.

Danny went back out on the field. He quickly lined up the offense and called out the signals.

"Hep! Hep! Hep!"

It was a draw play. Terry figured it out when he saw Jack Norbert, the fullback, move into handoff position. Sure enough, the offensive lineman pulled back as if to protect Danny for a pass. Seconds later, Jack moved up beside Danny. But to everyone's surprise, Terry had wormed his way through the line and was all over Danny like flypaper.

"Hey, you're getting it real fast," said Sid Keller. "Those Cougars better watch out for you on Saturday. You're going to make the rest of us look real good in the line."

Uh-huh, thought Terry. And if the coach needs me, I can still help out as a safety. I'm just going to be twice as useful to the team now.

"Go, Terry! Go!" came a shout from the stands as he lined up for the next play.

Nicky must have gotten through with his track practice early, Terry thought. I can always tell my number one fan by the piercing sound of his voice.

He glanced around to see if anyone else had heard the cry. Like Coach Butterfield, he thought nervously.

While those thoughts had run through his mind, Danny had gotten off the next play. Terry had completely missed his block, and the runner sped by him with no trouble at all.

"Wake up there, McFee," called the coach. "Danny, mix 'em up, but keep running those plays."

For the next half hour they went over and over and over the same three plays. Most of the time Terry was on top of things. But a lot of the time he wasn't. In fact, he was "pancaked" by the center more times than he cared to count. He just didn't seem to have the lineman's instincts.

When practice finally broke up, he mentioned this to John and Sid as they walked toward the locker room. "I guess I'm just used to having room to run and maneuver. Everything happens so *fast* on the front line. I don't know if I can react quickly enough."

"You might not have the instincts," said John.

"But you sure have the build."

"Nah, I belong in the secondary," said Terry.

"But your quickness will come in handy on the front line, too. You *did* sidestep Mike to get to Danny that one time, remember? Besides, I hate to tell you this, but not that many guys with your build are setting speed records," said Sid.

"Yeah, well, I can still leave you in the dust," said Terry. "Want to race me sometime?"

"Hey, I don't have to race you to know I'm not that fast at distances," said Sid. "But I'll still be in on the runner before your knuckles are off the ground."

"Take it easy, you guys," said John. "Let's face it — I'm the best there is at bringing down quarterbacks."

"Oh, yeah?" said Terry and Sid at the same time. They looked at each other and broke out in big smiles. "Let's hear it for Big Bad John, the meanest guy in town," said Sid.

"The Clippers' secret weapon," John agreed, tapping himself on the chest.

"The toughest dude in Clipperville!" said Sid.

"Avenger of the innocent," Terry offered, getting into the spirit of things.

" 'Bout time you guys recognized quality," said John, throwing mock punches at them.

"Can I have your autograph?" asked Terry, hiding his laughter behind his hand.

It was great being able to have a few laughs with the guys. Maybe defensive linemen weren't so different from any other players, he realized.

At the end of the last practice before the Cougars game, the coach announced the starting roster. Tony Glover would be going in as the free safety. Terry was listed as the starting nose tackle.

"I'm not sure I know all the plays, coach," Terry told him. "But I'll do my best."

"Can't ask for more than that," Coach Butterfield said.

There was a cold wind blowing, and the leaves were swirling down off the trees as the two McFee boys headed home that day.

Nicky was full of his adventures working out with

the track team. He went over every detail of every event for Terry's benefit. But Terry's mind really wasn't on what he was hearing. He was too busy thinking about tomorrow's game. He simply grunted or said "Uh-huh" every now and then. He figured it wouldn't make much difference to Nicky anyhow.

He was wrong. He realized Nicky's feelings were hurt when they had gone several blocks in complete silence.

Oh-oh, better do something about this, he thought.

"So, with all that stuff going on," he said, "how did you do in your events?"

"I told you," said Nicky. "I came in second twice and third once and I didn't get a chance to run again because practice ended."

"Wow! Two seconds and a third," said Terry. "You must be some pretty hot stuff!"

"Aw, gee," said Nicky, blushing. "I just like to run."

Terry looked down the block. They were about

fifty yards from their driveway, with no one in sight.

"You do? Okay, let's see if you can beat me to the driveway. Go!"

Caught off guard, even someone with Nicky's speed didn't have a chance. But he still managed to get there only a split second after Terry.

Puffing a little bit, Nicky shouted, "No fair! You knew we were going to race. I didn't."

Terry grabbed Nicky around the waist and started to rub his knuckles on top of his head, making his kid brother shake with laughter.

"Since when am I supposed to be fair? I'm older, remember? Come on, let's see if there's any of last night's cake left over."

There it was again. Terry felt a growling in his stomach, signaling that he was hungry. It always happened when he got home from school. He knew that a few cookies and a glass of milk wouldn't be enough.

Luckily there was half of a double-layer chocolate cake waiting for them.

By the time they finished their snack, there was only a small wedge left. Terry thought about finishing it, but remembered how much his father liked chocolate cake, too. Better leave some for him.

By this time, a heavy rain had started falling outside.

"Might as well do some homework," Terry said. "How about you, sport?"

"I'd rather be outside running," said Nicky.

"Well, you can't have what you want all the time," said Terry. "Besides, you'd better get used to running indoors. Once the weather gets real bad, that's where the track team practices, you know. You've got to be an all-around runner."

"I am," said Nicky. "I can beat you, too, when it's a fair race."

"Sure you can," said Terry, smiling to himself. He was a little surprised at the competitiveness in Nicky's voice. But he wasn't really worried about being outrun by his kid brother. Things hadn't gotten that bad.

But then Sid Keller's observation that guys with Terry's build — short legs and broad shoulders — rarely won races jumped into his mind.

Well, we'll see about *that*, Terry thought determinedly. I'll get my old speed back if I have to work out morning, noon, and night.

He looked over at Nicky to suggest that they schedule an early morning run. But Nicky was fast asleep.

Poor kid, Terry thought. He must be pooped from all the excitement. It'd probably be better for him to sleep in tomorrow. I'll just slip out before he's awake.

5

But the next morning Nicky caught up to Terry just as he was about to start his first lap.

"Why didn't you wake me up?" he asked. "Didn't you want me here?"

Terry, still groggy from the early morning hour, just grunted in reply. Nicky looked at him, then hesitatingly took his place beside him on the track.

The early morning sun had burned off most of the traces of the heavy downpour. By the time the two boys had reached the track, little wisps of fog were drifting off into the sky.

"I get to call, I get to call," said Nicky.

"Sure, no sweat," said Terry. Good thing he was getting a chance to loosen up before the game. He'd be ready for whatever those Cougars came up with. And once the coach saw how quickly he moved, he might even put him back in the safety slot.

With that in mind, Terry let Nicky win the first "race." Then he announced he was simply going to run some laps to warm up. Nicky could join in if he wanted, but it wasn't going to be a race.

"It's important to learn to pace yourself, too," Terry told him. "So we'll do three nice, steady laps and then call it a day. Okay?"

Nicky nodded. This wasn't the same as racing, but Terry could see that he was having fun anyhow.

They did their laps and came home to a kitchen filled with the smell of freshly made waffles.

"Your favorite pregame breakfast," announced Mrs. McFee.

"Great," said Terry. "But I'll just have a couple. Got to stay light on my feet!"

"Just two?" asked his mother.

"I'll have the rest of his," Nicky said. "I'm already light on my feet."

Lucky kid, Terry thought as he went up to his room.

A few hours later he came racing out of the locker room along with the rest of the Clippers in their navy blue and gold game uniforms. The Cougars, in red uniforms with white trim on the field. The Clippers' gold he brightly next to the Cougars' red ones.

There was no sign of yesterday's storm. Th was bright green with clear white chalk lines, air was cool and crisp, the sun shone brightly dow on the assembled crowd.

Terry went over to the side of the field where the defense usually worked out.

Russ Millick and Huey Page, the two corner-backs, were already slamming into each other, practicing their blocks.

"Come on, pal," called John Crum. "Make believe I'm a tough and mean Cougar runner."

"Sure," said Terry, knuckling down in a practice stance. "And I'll think of your nose as the football."

"Wise guy," said John, making a move toward him. But Terry slipped to one side, and John went flying by instead.

"You're going to be rockin' and a-rollin' today," said John, giving him a friendly tap on the shoulder pad.

whistle blew and the

national anthem. As

to relax and get rid of

r than ever to do so

The keys? What if I

' What if I get in the

.....ss up a play for another Clipper? *What if I'm just no good as a defensive lineman?*

All these questions rolled around in his mind as the coin toss took place at midfield.

The Cougars won and elected to receive. The Clippers would defend the goal on the north side of the field.

Frank Paulson, the substitute in the backfield for the Clippers, was also their placekicker. The defense lined up alongside of him. Terry took his place in the lineup.

At least this is one time I get a chance to race downfield, he thought, smiling.

The kick went high, then dropped down near the twenty-five-yard line, where it fell into the waiting arms of Sam Cutter, the Cougars' fullback. Since the Clippers' defensive wall was well on its way toward him, he signaled for a fair catch.

A few Clipper players left the field, while others came in. Terry stayed where he was. Coach Butterfield believed in using the power of his defensive line on a kickoff.

Mike Coolidge, a freckle-faced kid with sandy hair and a high, squeaky voice, was the quarterback for the Cougars. Terry had heard that although Mike didn't look that fierce, he was shrewd and could wear down a defense by constantly changing the attack.

Just what I need my first time in a new position, Terry thought.

The offensive huddle broke up, and the two teams lined up for the first play of the game from scrimmage.

In the distance, a high-pitched voice cut through the quiet in the stands and on the field.

"TER-REEEE!" came the familiar shout of encouragement from Nicky. It was nice to know there was one fan who didn't care which position he played.

Knuckles down, his legs set, Terry was all set to spring forward, to take control over José Fendez, the grim-faced Cougar center lined up opposite him.

"Ready! Set! Hep! Hep! Hep! Hep!"

Then, out of the corner of his eye, Terry saw the left guard pull back. Trap! flashed through his mind. Just as in practice. No time to wonder — he made his charge.

Pushing forward, he churned his legs under his body as he lifted Fendez clear into the air before he toppled over. Still pushing through the sea of blue and red uniforms swirling around him, Terry caught sight of the ballcarrier and lunged.

Sid Keller was aiming at the same target at the same time. The two Clipper linemen made contact one above the other in a cross tackle that caught Don Anderson, the Cougar ballcarrier, by complete surprise. The shock of the impact must have squeezed the ball from his grip, and it squirted forward.

There was a wild scramble for the ball. A stack

of Clippers and Cougars leaped on top of one another as the whistle blew.

When the officials managed to unpeel one player after another, the final color on top of the ball was navy blue and gold. The Clippers had recovered a fumble on the very first play of the game from scrimmage!

The crowd went wild.

Terry trotted off the field as the Clippers' offense took over on the Cougars' forty-yard line.

This is going to be a snap, he thought, looking up at the cheering crowd. He thought he saw his folks and Nicky near the forty-yard line, but mostly it was a blur.

"Nice block," said Tony Glover as they sat down on the bench to watch the offense. "You guys on the front line made my job pretty easy!"

"Thanks," said Terry. He tried not to let the fact that Tony was in *his* position dampen his spirits. "I hope it will be just the first of many good moves this game."

With the ball in good field position, Danny

played a conservative game. He kept it on the ground, moving the ball forward yard by yard until it was third and two on the twenty-yard line.

No mistakes, Danny. No mistakes. Terry could almost hear everyone on the bench thinking the same thing.

When the next play began, Danny drew to one side for a little screen pass to Sam Warren, his tight end. They'd run through the play about a hundred times in practice and always got it right. In the previous game, against the Skyhawks, they completed the same play six out of eight times. But not this time.

Just as Sam reached for the ball, his weight shifted a little too much over one foot, and he twisted his ankle. The ball bounced off his elbow just a few feet into the air, where it was grabbed by a Cougar linebacker.

Dazed by his good fortune, the lucky receiver hesitated for a moment. That was all it took for the alert Clipper right tackle to bring him down.

Another turnover. This time it meant that the defense would have to go to work.

"Go, Cougars! Go!"

The Cougars' fans were doing their best to cheer their team on.

You could see the determination of their offense when they came out of the huddle.

No long count here — the first play took place in a jiffy.

Terry made his block, but it didn't do much to prevent the pass. Mike Coolidge connected with his wide receiver, Rudy Dayton, for a gain of fifteen yards.

Tony should have covered that pass, Terry thought. I know I could have.

Wait a minute — he wasn't supposed to be thinking about pass coverage in the secondary. His job was in the line now.

He jogged over to his position on the defensive line and got ready for the next play.

The crowd had settled down, but Terry could still hear the distant sound of his name as Nicky shouted out his unflagging support: "TER-RREEEEE!"

Mike Coolidge had handed off to Don Anderson,

who broke through a hole in the line right next to Terry's left shoulder. Anderson spun free of the linebackers and broke across the field and down to the end zone for the first touchdown of the game. The Cougars went on the scoreboard, and after an easy kick through the uprights, it read: Cougars 7, Clippers 0.

The Clippers' offense took over after Russ Millick ran the ball back to the forty-yard line. But for the remainder of the period, it was slow progress toward the goal line, a few yards at a time as Danny kept the ball on the ground. When the team had finally made it to the twenty-five-yard marker, with third and seven, Danny connected with Sam Warren, his tight end, who carried the ball over the goal line.

The crowd roared, but the cheering soon turned to groans from the Clippers' fans. There was a flag down near the line of scrimmage. An offside penalty was called against the Clippers, nullifying Sam's touchdown.

The replay of the third down ended with the ball on the twenty-yard line. With fourth and two yards to go for a first down, Coach Butterfield signaled for the field goal team to take the field.

In his nice, clean uniform, Frank Paulson came out onto the field. Mike Randall snapped the ball back to Danny Stowe, who positioned it, and Frank kicked.

It was good. The Clippers went up on the scoreboard now, with three points next to their name, as the whistle blew to end the first quarter.

6

So far so good, thought Terry. At least I haven't done anything too dumb out there. He took a few deep breaths. Then he knelt down to watch Danny try to move the offense against a strong Cougar defense.

At the start of the second quarter, the Clippers' defense had done their job well. It took exactly three plays for them to force the Cougars to give up and punt the ball. Now Danny was attempting to take advantage of good field position. The Clippers had the ball on the Cougars' forty-yard line. It was first and ten.

"What do you think he'll do?" asked Sid Keller, kneeling next to Terry.

"Keep it on the ground, I suppose," Terry answered. "But I wish he'd go to the air."

"Yeah? Why?" Sid asked.

60

"Because their pass coverage isn't that great. See, watch that number seventeen. He hasn't done that much. So far, he's been lucky," said Terry. "Look, see how Dirk got by him?"

"You're right," said Sid. "Uh-oh, there goes the bomb!"

Danny had surprised the Cougars by firing a long bomb down to Dirk Solomon five yards from the goal line. Dirk grabbed it and sped across the line for a touchdown.

But the crowd's roar quickly turned to a moan. Dirk had stepped out of bounds, barely crossing over the sideline for an instant, and one of the officials had seen it. The pass was declared incomplete.

"It could have worked," said Terry. "Dirk had that safety beat by a mile."

"Boy, you sure do watch that safety position," said Chris Watkins, a Clipper linebacker. He'd overheard the conversation between Terry and Sid.

"I know," said Terry. "I played it long enough. I mean, since I was in the littlest football league, I always was fast. So I usually ended up in the defensive secondary. I . . . I never played in the line before."

"Yeah, but you'll do okay," said Chris. "You're big. . . ."

Big? Terry still couldn't get used to the idea of being described as big. Sometimes he felt like his body was growing right out of his clothes, but that was just because he was getting older, wasn't it?

Suddenly the defensive team was on its feet and running onto the field. The unsuccessful Clippers' offense came off and slogged down on the bench.

With the score still 7–3 in favor of the Cougars, the game was taking on the appearance of a ground war. Mike Coolidge called for one running play after another.

At first Terry seemed to be able to hold his own in the defensive line. He didn't key on the plays that quickly, but most of the time it didn't make all that much difference. The yardage was small, if steady.

About half the time he made his block. The rest

of the time he usually ended up on the ground. Once in a while he even managed to get in on a "red dog." He usually wasn't on the bottom of the pile, but he felt the punishing weight of all those above him.

As the game clock ground down toward the two-minute warning, both teams had stalled. When there was less than one minute to go, all Terry wanted was for the half to be over so he could collapse somewhere and nurse his bruises.

For what must have been the umpteen millionth time, he hunkered down at the line of scrimmage. Mike Coolidge had been brought down three times in the half — but he was still in there, calling the plays for the Cougars.

And José Fendez was still the man Terry had to contain or get by to help break up just about every play.

José looked real friendly most of the time. But when they lined up, he turned into a snarling jungle cat. That must be why he played for the Cougars, Terry realized.

"Cats! Set! Hut! Hut! Hut!" Coolidge called out.

At the start of the third "hut," Terry saw José begin to move forward. The Clippers' tackle was about to meet him head on when he sensed which way José would lean. By swerving slightly to the side, he caught his opponent off guard and slipped right by him. Dodging the blue and red uniforms surrounding him in their backfield, he made a lunge for the one with the ball tucked under his arm. It was Sam Cutter, the Cougars' fullback, looking to break away.

But just as he was about to make contact, Sam skipped off to one side, and Terry found himself hugging the ground. He scrambled up to his feet just in time to see the Cougar ballcarrier race down the field and cross the goal line.

The Cougars' kicking team took the field, and in a matter of seconds the scoreboard had changed to Cougars 14, Clippers 3.

In the remaining seconds of the half, after the Cougars had kicked the extra point, the Clippers had possession of the ball. The offense did its best but couldn't get it beyond the midfield stripe.

When they left the field, the totals on the score-board remained the same.

Coach Butterfield let his team catch its breath during the first few moments in the locker room. When they had settled down, he delivered his pep talk. The first thing he pointed out was that the score didn't tell the whole story.

"You scored once and you were scored on twice," said the coach. "No big deal. What's really important is how you're playing. Let's take it one at a time. Offense, you're missing out in a couple of ways. Tackles and guards, you're not opening up holes. Backfield, you're not finding them."

He went on to point out exactly which plays were working and which were not.

"Receivers, you have to run your patterns faster. Danny isn't getting all that much time to get off his passes."

Then he moved on to defense.

"I know we have some changes there," he said. "Mostly they're working out."

Mostly? thought Terry. Hold on. I'm the only

66

new guy in the line, and Tony's the only new guy in the secondary. Which one of us isn't doing that well?

He didn't have to wait long.

"Frankly, we've been lucky on a lot of plays. The line just isn't clicking yet. I suppose some of it's because you haven't played together that long. But each one of you has to pull his weight and get in there on some of those running plays before they break loose. Can't count on the backup to bring 'em down all the time. And they're getting too much ground yardage on us. It could start to hurt in the next half. Secondary, nice work. You're outrunning them and doing a job on their receivers. That ought to pay off now."

Terry thought that Tony had been doing a pretty good job, but it still hurt his pride to hear Tony singled out like that. He was used to coaches telling him what he'd just heard about Tony.

"Okay, now," said the coach, winding up his talk. "The thing you have to do this half is concentrate on what you're doing. And rev up the speed and pour on the power. Give it all you've got!"

Mike Randall, the center, led the cheer as they left the locker room.

"Go! Clippers! Go! Fight, team, fight!"

Their cleats echoed on the concrete floor as they made their way down the passage to the field. But when they burst out into the golden sunlight of the autumn day, they were greeted by an even louder roar from their fans.

Terry knew that one of the voices making up a lot of that noise came from Nicky. No matter what happened, he'd always have his kid brother in his corner.

It wasn't long into the second half before he needed some outside cheering. The Cougars had gotten possession of the ball at their own thirty. Mike Coolidge, with an eleven-point lead, had gotten a little cocky and tried some long passes. Thanks to the Clippers' secondary, he hadn't connected with most of them. Tony Glover and Don Payne, the strong safety, were covering the Cougar receivers like wallpaper.

But a lot of that was luck, too, Terry knew. And the fact that Mike Coolidge had time to get off those long bombs meant the defensive line had to start pushing even harder.

So far they had been held by a smart, tough Cougar offensive line.

During a time-out, Coach Butterfield called Chris Watkins, the defensive captain, and John Crum to the sideline.

When those two players returned to the defensive huddle, they passed on his instructions.

"Coach says we have to shape up the pass rush," said Chris. "Sid, Terry, he wants you guys to get in closer and take out your guys faster."

What does he think I'm trying to do? ran through Terry's mind. I'm pushin' and shovin' as hard and as fast as I can.

"We all have to move like lightning once the ball's snapped, too," added John. "Fast and hard, that's the way!"

"Okay!"

"Right!"

"Rah, Clippers!"

The defense cheered as their huddle broke up and they headed for the scrimmage line.

The ball was now on their forty-five-yard line. It was first and ten for the Cougars.

Terry tried to concentrate on what the guys had passed on from the coach. Get in there faster, that was the first thing.

He got into his stance opposite Fendez, who looked as mean as ever. Terry watched him like a hawk, waiting for him to snap the ball so he could bring him down.

As Coolidge barked out the signals, he was all poised to move.

"Het! Het! Het!"

That was it: He detected a flutter of motion — or at least he thought he did — and he sprang forward.

Whistles blew. Flags flew. Bodies scrambled to avoid connecting with one another.

In an instant, Terry knew what had happened.

"Offside!" shouted the ref.

A five-yard penalty against the Clippers — and it

was all his fault, Terry realized. Even worse, he had to do it right after they'd gotten a pep talk from the coach.

The Cougars got set on the forty, with only five to go for a first down.

"Take it easy," said Huey Page as the defense moved into position. "Plenty of time."

Sure, thought Terry. The coach is saying for us to move it, and Huey's telling me to relax!

As Coolidge moved into position behind his center, the stands were quiet. But as soon as he started barking out his signal, a piercing shout came sailing across the field.

"TER-REEEEE!"

José Fendez snickered nastily and snapped the ball. The little bit of time it took Terry to recover his concentration was all the Cougars needed. Terry completely missed his block, and their offensive line held. Coolidge had all the time in the world to set himself in position for the long bomb.

Don Payne had done his best all day trying to hold down Rudy Dayton, the Cougars' wide receiver, but not this time. Dayton snagged the ball

71

on the ten-yard line and practically strolled into the end zone for their third touchdown of the day.

It's all my fault, thought Terry. It's all my fault.

He could hardly lift his head as he trotted down the field to line up for the extra-point kick.

None of the other Clipper defensemen said much to him. Instead they were concentrating on trying to block the kick. It might help out on the scoreboard later.

But the kick was clean and straight down the middle.

The scoreboard now read: Cougars 21, Clippers 3.

It's turning into a runaway, Terry thought, and it's because of me.

"McFee, come over here," called Coach Butterfield from the corner of the bench. "Sit down and cool off."

Cool off? I'm as dead cold as an ice cube, Terry thought. I just wish I could get hot out there!

But he sat down quietly where the coach had pointed and didn't say a word out loud. Instead, he just watched the game silently.

It looked like Danny had gotten his second wind. He began by moving the team with a series of short passes and running plays that gained a little more yardage each time. Then, when the Cougars' defense least suspected it, he unleashed the long bomb and connected with Sam Warren, the tight end, who was all by himself right next to the goal line.

And almost as quickly, the team kicked the extra point with no trouble at all.

For the second time that day, the cheers rang out as the Clippers went up on the scoreboard, making it read: Cougars 21, Clippers 10.

Terry added it up — it would now take two TDs to win the game, but there was still plenty of time to do it.

He grabbed his helmet and started to leave the bench when the coach signaled him to stay put.

At the opposite end of the bench, he saw Tony Vail, the substitute nose tackle, get up and trot off to join the Clippers on the field. In his clean uniform, everyone could see that someone new was in there now.

Terry's heart sank.

He'd been left on the bench before. Lots of times the coach replaced players so they could get some rest or recover from a strong hit or something. But he knew that wasn't the case this time. He knew he was out of the game because he wasn't pulling his weight.

Maybe the coach figures I'm just not up for playing on the line, he thought. Well, that's just fine with me. Because as soon as this game is over, I'm going to work on my speed. And I'm going to get back my old job.

7

The Clippers' defense — without Terry McFee playing — managed to hold off the Cougars for the rest of the third quarter. Neither team got close enough to threaten, and the score remained the same going into the final period.

As the two teams reversed field position, Coach Butterfield glanced over at Terry.

"How are you doing, McFee?" he asked.

Terry nodded his head. "Okay," he said.

"I think I was pushing you too hard in there," said the coach. "Too much for you to learn all at once. You just watch for a while and you'll get the hang of it. You'll be fine, so don't worry about not playing the full game. Maybe I'll put you in a little later."

Terry didn't know what to think. On the one hand, he was glad the coach hadn't written him off as a complete wuss. But on the other, he wasn't sure he wanted to "get the hang" of the nose tackle position — at least not if it meant giving up his old free safety position to Tony Glover for good!

In the final quarter, Danny Stowe teamed up with his two favorite receivers, Dirk Solomon and Sam Warren, to move the ball down to the thirty-five-yard line. The Cougars held them off for two downs by breaking up pass plays that could have gone the distance. But on third and ten, Danny surprised them by throwing a quick lateral pass to Jack Norbert, the Clippers' fullback, who broke loose and carried the ball across the goal line.

After the conversion, with about five minutes to go, the scoreboard read: Cougars 21, Clippers 17.

"Four points. Only four points. We need another touchdown," said Frank Paulson, sitting next to Terry on the bench.

The crowd roared its encouragement.

"Get that ball! Get that ball!"

"Hey, hey, what do you say — take the ball the other way!"

One thing was for sure: The Clippers' fans were louder than the Cougars' rooters.

With the score that close, Terry knew the coach wouldn't take any chances. Sure enough, he kept his new defensive tackle on the bench.

Even without him, the Clippers' defense was having trouble holding off the Cougars' attack. Both teams were tired and made mistakes, but the ball continued to move forward down the field.

For one moment, though, it looked like the big break the Clippers needed would finally happen.

With eight yards to go for a first down, on the twenty-five-yard line, Coolidge threw a short screen pass to his flanker, Jay Reese. Russ Millick had made a move in that direction, threw up his hand, and tipped the ball before it reached its destination. It bobbled up in the air and came down into the waiting arms of Chris Watkins.

Barely glancing around for daylight, Watkins started to rush forward when he was brought down by the Cougars' right guard. It all happened so fast and unexpectedly, Watkins lost his grip, and the ball rolled forward.

There was a mad scramble and an instant pileup in the middle of the field on top of the ball. But when the bodies were unpeeled, the final form pressed down on the ball was wearing a Cougar uniform.

Terry knew that it was at times like this that you couldn't give up. He also knew how disappointing it was when a big break didn't come through, after all.

Maybe that's why the remaining minutes of the game saw little real movement by either side. The Clippers tried to summon up some pep, but they just didn't have it. Luckily, the Cougars weren't playing at their best by that time, either.

But by the end of the game the Cougars had won, largely by their efforts in the first three quarters.

As a dejected Clipper team scrambled into the locker room, Coach Butterfield tried to cheer them up.

"A few mistakes we can easily fix," he said. "All in all, most of you played a really good game. But we have our work cut out for us. Get some rest and I'll see you at practice next week."

Terry got cleaned up and dressed quickly. While some of the others hung around the locker room talking over the game, he left quietly and walked toward the parking lot. He could see his mother and father talking to some of the other parents, while Nicky sat up on the fender of Mrs. McFee's gray station wagon. For a moment Terry thought of slipping back into the locker room, but Nicky had already spotted him.

"Terry!" called the younger boy. He slipped down from the fender and dashed across the driveway in Terry's direction.

"Nicky!" cried Mrs. McFee. "Stop!"

But Nicky had already reached his brother and thrown his arms around him.

"Nicky! Don't you ever run off like that without looking in both directions first!" Mrs. McFee scolded him.

"Your mother's right," added Mr. McFee. "You have to be careful, Nicky."

Nicky looked down at the ground. "I just wanted to see Terry," he said. "I wanted to—"

Mrs. McFee took hold of Nicky and walked off to one side of the road with him. From a distance it looked as though she were having a serious talk to explain what he had done wrong.

"It's okay, Nicky," said Terry when they returned to the car. "I just want to go home."

"Let's all get in the car," said Mr. McFee. "You drive," he said to his wife.

The two boys piled in the backseat.

"How come you stopped playing?" Nicky asked Terry as soon as their seat belts were buckled. "Didn't you want to play anymore? Danny played the whole game as the quarterback. Jack played the whole game as the fullback. Ray played the whole game as the left tackle. Sid played the whole game on the left side. Huey played the whole game—" Nicky pointed out.

"Okay! Okay! Some of the guys are set in their positions. Listen, can we talk about something else?" Terry snapped.

There was silence in the car for the next several minutes.

Finally, Mrs. McFee spoke up. "I thought we might manage one last cookout before we put away the grill for the season. I have some hot dogs and hamburgers and coleslaw, but we don't have your favorite, Terry."

"Potato salad!" Nicky piped up.

"We could pick some up at the market. It's on our way," said his mother.

"I . . . I don't really want any," said Terry. He loved it and usually ate tons of it whenever he could. "I'm not that hungry."

"And after a game?" asked Mrs. McFee. "You usually eat like a horse — win or lose. I wonder if you're coming down with something."

"No, I feel fine," said Terry. "I just don't seem to have an appetite right now."

Terry had only one hot dog and one hamburger that evening. And he didn't load up his plate with a lot of other things. Nicky, on the other hand, ate

81

three hot dogs and had two big helpings of cole-slaw, along with nonstop nibbling on the crinkly potato chips Mr. McFee had dug out of the back of the cupboard.

"Nicky, you're going to explode," said Mr. Mc-Fee. "You're not going to be able to run upstairs, never mind around a track."

"Want to see?" asked Nicky. "I can do it."

"No, I'm just kidding," said his father. "I'm sure you'll burn it off before your next practice. Your coach says he's never seen someone with your energy and enthusiasm." He shot Terry a quick look. "Seems I remember a time when that could be said about *both* my boys."

Mrs. McFee interrupted before he could go on. "Who wants to help me carry these things inside?" she asked. "Terry? Can you give me a hand?"

"Sure, Mom," he said. He piled a stack of plates in one hand and grabbed a jar of pickles with the other.

When they got into the kitchen, Mrs. McFee took the pickle jar from him.

"I'm not going to bug you, Terry, by asking

what's wrong. I'm sure you're disappointed that you didn't play the whole game," she said. "But I know that you'll work that out. I just want to tell you that if there's anything bothering you, well, you know you can always talk to me. Or to your father. Or even to Nicky."

Terry almost blurted out that he felt like the biggest loser on the football team. That he couldn't block or rush or tackle or do any of the things a defensive lineman was supposed to do. That he'd disappointed the coach. And that he wasn't so sure he could move fast enough to get his old position back.

But it seemed so silly. It didn't sound like that big a deal. His folks would probably pat him on the back and tell him just to do the best he could. Things would work out.

Well, they were going to work out, because he was going to make them. He was going to practice his running and his moves on his own so he could play safety again. All he had to do was work a little harder.

So he kept his problem to himself. He simply

said, "Thanks, Mom, I know it. I'll be okay. You know what? I don't think I want to watch Nicky's movie tonight. I think I'll hit the hay."

"Okay," Mrs. McFee said. "I'll explain to Nicky why you aren't watching with us. He'll be disappointed because — well, never mind." She looked as if she wanted to say something more, but instead she just kissed him good night.

8

The next morning, Terry awoke while it was still dark outside. He looked over at the alarm clock with its glow-in-the-dark digital numbers and saw that it was at least an hour before anyone else would be up — especially on a Sunday morning.

Great — I'll get in a run before anyone even misses me, he thought.

That's when he heard it — the steady sound of something tapping on the window.

He raised the window shade and saw the wet-streaked window, the raindrops slowly sliding down the moment they made contact.

Rats! Rotten weather, the one thing I hadn't counted on.

He climbed back into bed and tried to fall asleep. Instead, he kept thinking of numbers and

85

play combinations. First he ran through the new way he had to learn them from the nose tackle's position. Then he went back to the way it was when he played safety. They were the same plays, just different ways of looking at them.

Maybe that's where the trouble was. He just couldn't give up all that he had learned in his years as a free safety. Not without a fight.

He leaped out of bed and stripped off his pajama top. Staring at himself in the mirror above his bureau, he flexed his arm muscles. Not bad, he thought. Plenty of strength there.

He did some twists and turns, quietly, so he wouldn't wake anyone else. Then he lay on his back and did a few bicycles before settling in for the hard work.

Locking his toes under the sideboard of his bed, he clasped his hands behind his back and slowly raised his upper body to a sitting position.

"One," he whispered, breathing out as he twisted one elbow in, followed by the other. Then he flopped back and repeated the procedure.

"Two." Breath. "Three." Breath. "Four."

He had reached twenty before he realized there was someone standing behind him.

Glancing over his shoulder, he saw baggy flannel pajama pants sagging around the ankles — a dead giveaway for Nicky.

"Whatcha doin'?" asked the younger boy.

"Trying to get back into shape," said Terry. He huffed and puffed as he continued to do his sit-ups.

"You're in shape," said Nicky. "You can play football. I can't."

"Sure you can," said Terry, stopping his exercise and lying back on the floor. "You're just better at other things. Like running."

"I'm going to be in the Olympics," Nicky announced.

"Right, and I'm going to be in the Super Bowl!" Terry hooted.

"I am! I am!" Nicky yelled. He jumped up and down.

Terry reached over and grabbed him around the

knees. Nicky tumbled, and the two of them began wrestling on the floor.

The noise woke Mrs. McFee, who came running into the room.

"Quiet, you two!" she whispered loudly. "You'll wake your father."

But Mr. McFee appeared right behind her in the doorway, rubbing his eyes.

"What's going on here?" he asked.

"I'm going to be in the Olympics!" Nicky said. "Terry doesn't believe me. Tell him! Tell him! I am!"

"Take it easy, Nicky," said his father. "It's true — sort of."

"What do you mean?" asked Terry.

"Let's have some breakfast and I'll explain," said Mr. McFee.

Sitting around the kitchen table a few minutes later, Mrs. McFee asked, "Have we all calmed down now?"

The two boys nodded their heads.

"Okay," said Mr. McFee. "Nicky was saving it to

tell you as a surprise after your game yesterday. But you didn't seem interested in talking about anything, or even hearing what anyone else said. So we decided to wait until today."

"Except that we didn't expect today to start so early," added Mrs. McFee. "The plan was for Nicky to bring you up your orange juice and tell you at the same time."

"Tell me what?" asked Terry.

"Nicky has been selected as one of the school's representatives for the Special Olympics!" said Mrs. McFee.

"I told you!" said Nicky.

Terry suddenly remembered Ms. Phillips, the track coach, mentioning something about that. He grinned.

"The Special Olympics, wow! So my little brother really is 'going for the gold'!" he said.

"Of course, he has to qualify in the 'indoor games' first," Mr. McFee added. "But it's an honor just to be selected at any level."

Terry recalled that the Special Olympics were

going to be held the next summer, but that there was going to be a midyear warm-up, the "indoor games," in midwinter.

"My coach says I have to practice real hard," Nicky told Terry seriously. "Want to help me practice?"

Terry thought for a moment. "Listen, Nicky," he said finally. "You've got a great coach to help you get ready. But I have to do my serious running on my own time. So I'm working out a new early morning schedule for myself. You can join me if you want to, but don't expect me to be able to help you out too much. I've got to concentrate on my own running. Okay?"

Nicky nodded, his head bowed. "Okay," he whispered.

Terry rubbed his knuckles across Nicky's head. "Great," he said. He tried to reassure himself that Nicky really was okay.

After all, he reasoned, the kid *does* have a real coach. And it's not like we won't be running together still. It'll just be a little different, that's all.

❋   ❋   ❋

Monday morning was bright and sunny. When the two McFee boys left for the cinder practice track, the warmth of the early morning sunshine wrapped itself around them. Sweat suits were shed before they took their first lap.

Nicky kept up with Terry, who had worked out a fixed schedule of training. Each day he would increase the number of laps and try to shorten the timing.

But on this first day, Terry didn't bother checking his stopwatch. He ran for the sheer joy of an early fall morning and his own pleasure.

When they started their final laps, Nicky sprinted ahead, challenging Terry to follow.

"No racing! Just steady laps," Terry called over to him.

Reluctantly, Nicky dropped back and returned to the same pace as his brother. They finished their run for that morning side by side and flopped down on the dewy grass to calm their breathing to normal.

"That was fun," said Nicky in a matter of seconds.

Terry hadn't recovered as quickly. He was still panting when Nicky started his cool-down exercises. Muscles aching slightly, Terry grunted as he got up and began his own routine.

His track coach was right — that kid has a lot of energy! he thought. He ought to do really well in the Special Olympics.

In the back of his mind was the nagging thought, I hope I do as well at reaching my goal!

All that week, the McFee brothers were regular workout partners in the early morning hours. Nicky soon got the message that Terry didn't want to race and settled down to doing laps with him. Even on the way home, they didn't break down and race the final distance to the house. As far as Terry was concerned, everything was working out just fine.

He barely noticed that Nicky's usual chatter had slowly died as the week went on.

Throughout the week, Terry practiced with the Clippers in the defensive tackle slot. He did his job and, one by one, he learned all the old plays from that position. But he never lost track of what the safety did on the same plays. And even though it was none of his business, he kept track of what the safety's job was when the coach outlined a few new plays.

But even as he worked to regain his speed, he realized something he hadn't wanted to admit before: He had the tremendous upper-body strength a good nose tackle needed.

One evening, when he and Nicky were roughhousing after throwing a football back and forth in the backyard, his little brother howled in pain.

"What's the matter?" Terry asked, releasing Nicky right away.

"You hurt me!" Nicky said, pouting.

"Didn't mean to," said Terry. He really hadn't. It seemed to him that he didn't do anything different than the two of them had done playing a million times before.

"Tell you what," he said as the little guy rubbed his shoulder. "I'll let you pick the Saturday night movie *again.*" That should put things straight, he thought.

Terry got a chance to test the results of his conditioning the following Saturday. The Clippers played an away game against the Rhinos, the toughest team in the league the previous year.

As usual, Coach Butterfield read off the roster in the locker room before the game. There were no surprises. Terry hadn't expected any. He was still in at defensive tackle. Tony was still in the free safety slot.

It's okay. I'll just do my job and help out the team as best I can. But if Tony doesn't measure up, then maybe the coach will see that I'm fast enough again for the job.

With that in mind, he raced onto the field with the rest of the team. He came within a whisker of overtaking Dirk, who usually emerged at the head of the pack.

During the warm-up, Terry threw himself into getting ready. Going through all the usual drills with the rest of the guys, he was always about a half second ahead. When he was supposed to be waiting his turn to throw a block or run a lap, he danced in place.

By the time the game started, he could hardly sit on the bench.

"What's gotten into you?" asked Dex Gorten, one of the Clippers' linebackers. "You trying out for All-American?"

Terry laughed. "Can't start too early."

Danny Stowe and Hank McGraw, the Rhinos' captain, waited out in the middle of the field for the coin toss. McGraw was unusually tall. In his bright orange uniform with the green trim, he reminded Terry of a carrot. But a carrot who is smart and can really throw that pigskin, he remembered from last year.

McGraw called out loudly, "Tails!"

But the coin had landed heads up. Danny told the ref the Clippers would receive.

The offensive team took to the field, and Terry finally sat down.

As he watched his own team gradually move the ball downfield, Terry kept his eye on the Rhinos' defense. Were they doing anything special?

It didn't look it. They just seemed to do everything right. Danny managed to gain about twenty yards before the Clippers got stuck on the line of scrimmage at their own forty-yard line. With fourth and ten, they had no choice but to punt the ball to the Rhinos.

Terry put on his helmet and ran out to his position on the punting team. By this time he knew exactly where he was supposed to be and what moves he had to make once he spotted the runner.

But the kick was high and not that deep. It landed in the hands of Pat Miller, the Rhinos' fullback, on their thirty-five-yard line. He signaled for a fair catch. There was no chance to bring him down on that play.

McGraw took only a few seconds in their huddle to rally the Rhino offense for their first play of the game.

Terry got into his position in the Clippers' line and listened to McGraw bark out his signals.

"Ready! Five! Six! Seven! Hike!"

The ball was snapped back to McGraw, who

spun around and slapped it into Pat Miller's stomach.

At the same time, Terry had sprung forward and thrown a block at the huge Rhino center trying to prevent him from getting through. With his split-second timing, Terry had managed to outsmart his opponent. The larger player crumbled as Terry twisted by.

But a hole had opened farther down the line, and Miller had seen it. He dashed through and broke away for a gain of about fifteen yards. Russ Millick, the Clippers' right cornerback, knocked him out of bounds just shy of the midfield stripe.

On the next play, the Rhinos took the ball across the halfway mark and into Clippers' territory. That was followed by three short pass plays that gained them another first down. They were now on the forty and threatening.

After each play, Terry faithfully jogged back to his position in the line. He wasn't sure, but he figured he was a split second faster than the center who was blocking him. In a couple of plays he almost got a piece of McGraw before he got the pass

off. He was determined to bring down the Rhino quarterback at least once before the half.

While the Rhinos' offense was moving forward, Terry also noticed that Tony Glover was covering his receivers just the way he should. Can't count on Tony to mess up, he thought. Oh, well, maybe he'll wear out and the coach will have to find someone who knows the plays to take over.

When the Rhinos had moved the ball down to the thirty-five-yard line, Coach Butterfield signaled Chris Watkins, the defensive captain, to call for a time-out.

The coach gathered the defensive team around at the sideline.

"You guys really have to dig in here," he said. "If they score this early in the game, there's a chance they'll run away with it. Huey, you're missing your coverage. Lots of opportunities for you to get in there. Terry, you're hitting — but you're not hitting hard enough. Big, husky guy like you, let 'em know it! Chris, you're dragging your tail. Pep it up back there. . . ."

He ran through the whole defensive team, pointing out their shortcomings one after another. Then he said, "I know you guys have the stuff. Now show it to me!"

"Rah! Clippers! Go team! Go!"

Chris tried to keep the spirit alive. He patted most of the guys on the back as they ran onto the field.

As they lined up behind the ball, Terry could feel the heat. Beads of sweat trickled down the back of his neck. He shook it off and crouched down.

McGraw barked out the signals. It seemed forever before Terry detected the slightest bit of motion. And then he made his move.

A whistle shrieked and the play collapsed.

Offside!

The ref's handkerchief stared him in the eye.

Just what they didn't need at this point.

John Crum sidled over to him and said, "Take it easy there, big guy."

It could happen to anyone. In fact, most of the guys were offside at least a couple of times a season. Still, he felt like a nerd. This was his second game in the defensive line. By this time he should have had a better sense of timing.

"TER-REEEEE!"

Nicky's cry was followed by a wave of laughter from the stands. Terry felt his neck get hot.

He's reminding everyone that the penalty was my fault, Terry thought. Well, let's hope he has something good to cheer about soon.

At the start of the next play, Freddie Mann, the Rhinos' center, was offside. With two penalties in a row, the crowd was growing restless. Cheers mixed with loud boos.

Both teams seemed mired in one spot.

From his experience playing in the backfield, Terry knew that this was a dangerous time. Play could get real sloppy, and anything could happen. He reminded himself about that as he took his place in the line.

Careful not to jump the gun, he lowered his head and waited for the play to begin.

"Hut! Hut! Hut!" McGraw called out.

At the first sign of motion, Terry plunged ahead, raising his body and tossing Freddie Mann to one

101

side. He almost broke through, but Pete Perez, the left tackle, just managed to bring him down with a well-placed shoulder.

The scramble in the line gave McGraw the time he needed. He threw a bullet pass to his wide receiver at the five-yard line, and a few seconds later, the Rhinos were on the scoreboard.

McGraw himself kicked the point after, and the Rhinos' lead was up there for everyone to see: 7–0.

"TER-REEEEE!"

This time Nicky's yell got a response from the Rhinos' fans. A sarcastic chant of "Terry, Terry, Terry" rose from the opposing team's stands.

That does it, Terry thought angrily. As if I'm not having enough trouble out here as it is! I'm going to have to get the message through to that kid once and for all — tonight!

The remainder of the first half saw no change in the score. One after another, the two teams inched their way ahead. But after no more than two sets of downs, each was forced to give up the ball.

There were no turnovers. The few fumbles that

took place were recovered by the team that made them. No passes were intercepted.

"It's real grind-it-out ball," said Terry, sitting on the bench next to Sid Keller.

"I hate it," said Sid. He grinned and gave Terry a sly look. "But at least *you're* getting some fan recognition!"

The whistle blew before Terry could offer a retort. The first half had ended.

Coach Butterfield tried to instill some pep into his team during halftime.

He held his thumb and forefinger a tiny bit apart. "You're just that far from getting there," he told them. "Just a little more effort and you're going to start scoring, offense. Defense, you guys have to put out a little more effort, too. You're all doing most everything right. You're better than they are, all in all. Let's see you prove it out there."

9

Terry joined the others in the dash out to the field. He yelled and cheered along with everyone else.

But his heart wasn't in it.

For all the good I'm doing, I might as well take a seat on the bench, he thought. If only the coach would give me a shot at safety, I know I could keep the Rhinos from scoring again!

The Clippers' offense came alive, though, in the second half. In two successive downfield marches, Danny brought them within scoring position. But each time, a turnover cost them their chance.

First Sam Warren forgot his pattern and turned the wrong way. A Rhino safety intercepted and ran the ball out of bounds. That led to a Rhino field goal, bringing the score to 10–0 in their favor.

Later, Danny couldn't find a receiver and had elected to run with the ball. Two Rhino linemen brought him down with such force, he lost the ball. In the scramble for the fumble, a Rhino tackle had recovered the ball. Another Rhino push toward the goal produced another field goal.

The offense's near-misses were heartbreaking — but the defense's play was looking sad, plain and simple. At the start of the fourth and final quarter, they had been scored upon three times.

"TER-REEEE!"

And every time Nicky's voice rang out, Terry wanted to disappear into his cleats.

The teams exchanged sides, and Terry dragged himself up from the bench to cheer on Danny and the Clippers' offense. They had just taken over the ball on their own thirty-yard line.

"Come on, Danny! Let's go, you Clippers!" Terry shouted. Even if he wasn't doing that much good, he hoped the offense could make the difference in the final period.

"Two TDs! Two TDs!"

His voice was almost drowned out amid the cheers of the Clippers' fans.

Maybe all that cheering was the spark they needed. Terry watched with growing hope as Danny led the Clippers downfield. When they got to the Rhinos' thirty-yard line, though, they seemed to get stuck again.

It was fourth and ten, and Coach Butterfield signaled for the field-goal attempt.

The two teams lined up. Mike snapped the ball back, but there was a bobble trying to place it.

The Rhinos rushed in, but Danny managed to scoop up the ball before they could get near it.

The Clippers' quarterback saw daylight to the right side of the field and made a break for it.

He dodged by the only Rhino nearby and sped downfield and across the goal line.

Finally, the Clippers were on the scoreboard! They made no mistakes booting the ball for the extra point, so the score now read: Rhinos 13, Clippers 7.

"Get that ball!"

"*Defense!*"

"TER-REEEEEE!"

The cheers rang out as the Clippers' defense took to the field. They had to hold the Rhinos and, if possible, grab hold of the ball.

After a quick huddle, McGraw took his position behind Freddie Mann, the center. Terry lined up opposite. Fired up by the Clippers' touchdown, he hunkered down and gave Freddie his nastiest snarl. He thought he saw Freddie's eyes widen in surprise for a moment, but then the quarterback started to call the signals, and the center dropped his gaze.

So, thought Terry, *that's* how things work here on the line! That's something you miss in the backfield. I'll have to remember to try a little friendly intimidation from now on.

As these thoughts sped through his mind, the play began — and he was a little slow making his move. The opposing lineman caught him off balance and flattened him.

That gave McGraw the time he needed. He threw a long, high pass to his wide receiver down in enemy territory.

Tony Glover had followed the pattern and was

right there with his target. As the ball came toward him, he reached up to block it and nicked it with his fingertip.

Russ Millick was nearby and flew after it before it could hit the ground. He grabbed it while he was still on his feet and managed to dance out of bounds just before a slew of Rhinos got to him.

As the fans shouted and tossed confetti into the air, the Clippers' offense started to rush onto the field.

That was when someone noticed that Tony hadn't gotten up from the ground. Terry could see him trying to move, but falling back in obvious pain. He rushed over to see what had happened.

Coach Butterfield and the team trainer beat him to it. Terry could only stand there and watch as they examined Tony.

Finally, they signaled Terry and Sid to come over to help their teammate off the field.

"Looks like a bad sprain," said the coach. "We'll get some ice on it right away."

Tony was ash white and silent as he hobbled off the field with their help. They brought him into the locker room and left him with the trainer. Then they rushed back to see what was happening in the final few minutes of the game.

Danny was playing it safe. He kept the ball on the ground, using his offensive backfield for all it was worth.

It seemed as though the Clippers would have one more chance to score before the clock ran out.

They were on the forty, with second and ten, when they got a lucky break.

Danny had handed the ball off to Jack Norbert, who tried to run through a hole in the left side of the line. But the Rhinos put up a wall and he went crashing backward. The ball slipped out of his hand, and Danny grabbed it.

None of the Rhinos was covering the Clippers' quarterback by then, and he was in the clear. For the second time that day, he carried the ball across the goal line for a Clipper touchdown.

For the second time, the Clippers kicked for the extra point and made it.

They were now ahead of the Rhinos by one point. There was less than a minute left to play.

When it was time for the defense to take to the field, Coach Butterfield turned to Terry and said, "McFee, you'll have to go in as safety. No one else knows the plays. Tony Vail, let's see what you can do as nose tackle. Remember, they're not out of it until the whistle blows. Do everything you can to wear them down — and run out that clock!"

Terry knew the coach was desperate. Tony Vail hadn't played defense since their first practice.

Still, when Terry took to the field he felt like singing. He was going to be playing his old position. The coach hadn't completely written him off as a speed merchant. This was where all those mornings of running were going to pay off. All he had to do was get through the next minute of play. Then, later on, he could talk to the coach about going back to the safety position on a permanent basis.

As the Rhinos got set to begin play, Chris Watkins gathered the defensive team for a quick huddle.

"Do your job, but remember to play through. Not everyone knows all the plays, so we have to help each other out. Let's clobber 'em!"

The two teams leaped into position at the line of scrimmage. The ball was on the Rhinos' thirty-five-yard line.

With so little time, Terry knew McGraw would have to pass. Terry would have to keep his wits about him and anticipate the long bomb.

McGraw did what was expected of him. He threw a series of quick, short passes for a few yards at a time. Each time, the receiver got the ball and stepped or ran out of bounds to stop the clock. The Rhinos were inching forward, second by second. And so far, the defensive line hadn't been able to stop them.

Despite himself, Terry kept thinking about what Tony should have been doing. The big lineman didn't let anyone get by him — but he didn't make any headway against the passer, either.

For the first time, Terry began to see that playing tackle wasn't all a matter of bulk — it took some brains, too.

But dancing around the backfield, waiting for the next play, he felt that this was where he belonged. This was where he could really show his stuff.

He managed to hold his own against the Rhinos' best receiver, Joe Rushing, who had fingertips like suction cups. So far, Terry had outrun him on each play — even though the ball hadn't come that way yet.

Then, with third and ten, and only a few seconds left on the clock, McGraw unleashed the bomb. He sent a bullet flying downfield to Rushing, who was within twenty yards of the goal.

At first, Terry was right there with him. The two players raced together almost side by side.

But suddenly Rushing put on a burst of speed.

Terry churned his legs as hard and as fast as he could, but it was no use.

Rushing snagged the ball and raced across the goal line as the whistle blew to end the game.

The Rhinos had won, 19–14.

It took every ounce of strength Terry had to drag his body off the field and into the locker room.

10

Terry was silent the whole ride home and all through dinner. But after dinner, he had a serious talk with Nicky. He tried to explain that all that shouting didn't always help. When it came at the wrong time, it made him uncomfortable. Sometimes it bothered him and made him forget what he was doing. In fact, although he didn't mention it, he couldn't help wondering if it might have been partially Nicky's fault that he hadn't done all that well when he went back to the safety position.

Nicky was crushed. His normally cheerful face turned pale, and his lower lip drooped. Terry could tell that he was on the edge of tears.

"It's not like you did something bad on purpose, Nicky," he explained. "I'm not mad at you. I just don't want you yelling like that during games, okay?"

That seemed to do the trick. Nicky brightened up a little and nodded.

Terry wished he could change moods that easily. It tore him up inside to know that he'd let the team down. But even worse was the thought that he'd finally been given the chance to play safety again — and he'd blown it.

The following morning, when Nicky came to get him for his run, Terry told him he had a headache and couldn't go.

On Monday morning, he said his knee hurt him.

On Tuesday, he claimed he was coming down with a cold.

By Wednesday, Nicky had stopped asking him. In fact, Nicky had stopped going for an early morning run, too. Terry never even noticed.

Terry showed up at football practice on Thursday.

"Feeling a little better?" the coach asked. "Think you're up for working out with the team today?"

Over the past few days, Terry had thought a lot about whether to quit playing football that season. After all, he could start all over next year.

But he knew it would be too painful to spend the rest of the season completely away from his favorite sport. He knew that even playing tackle was better than nothing. Besides, if he just minded his own business and did what he was told, he'd keep a place on the team. After the season, he could start getting back into shape for a tryout at the safety position.

"I'm fine, coach," he said. "I'll just go over there and work on my blocking with the rest of the line."

"Right," said Coach Butterfield. "But don't push too hard. Work yourself back gradually. A husky, healthy fella like you, well, you're going to do just fine."

The coach's words were encouraging, but they did little to boost Terry's black mood. He did a passably good job in the defensive tackle spot that practice. Once in a while he broke through and stopped the pass. Once in a while he brought down the runner. Once in a while he helped break up a play.

But as far as he was concerned, nothing could match the thrill of beating a receiver to the ball, of anticipating the long bomb — and getting there first. He couldn't help wondering if he'd ever feel that kind of excitement again. Was there anything about the nose tackle position that could equal it? he wondered.

Because he had missed three days of practice that week, Terry spent the first half of Saturday's game against the Rangers on the bench. At first he didn't pay very much attention to what was happening on the field. But he loved football too much to ignore the game going on in front of him for long. Soon he was cheering and yelling support along with the rest of the team.

Midway through the first quarter, Terry got a shock. As the defensive team readied themselves for the play, he caught himself watching one player more closely than anyone else. And that player wasn't Tony Glover. It was Josh Hansen, the Clippers' substitute nose tackle.

He's standing too high off the ground, he thought. He's going to get pancaked if he doesn't watch it!

And sure enough, moments after the ball was snapped, Josh was flattened. The center practically lifted him off his feet before throwing him to the ground.

Terry found himself observing the Rangers' nose tackle, too. That player lined up so close to Mike Randall that his helmet seemed to touch the Clippers' center.

I'll bet he's able to get the jump on Mike, Terry thought. Either that, or he's working on his intimidation!

Seconds later, Mike was sitting on his rear end and the Rangers' tackle was bringing Danny down.

It was the end of the first half before either team scored. Then, amid loud cheers from the Clippers' fans, Dirk Solomon crossed the goal line, carrying the ball like a loaf of bread. The bench slapped high fives and cheered lustily as the offensive team lined up for the extra point. Frank Paulson, the Clippers' placekicker, positioned the ball and stepped in for the kick.

But the ball had barely connected with his toe

when a Ranger player leaped high into the air — and slapped the ball down.

Terry's jaw dropped. The Ranger player who had thwarted their extra point was the nose tackle!

Just then the whistle blew, signaling the end of the first half. The Clippers were ahead, 6–0. Coach Butterfield's pep talk was full of praise.

"Don't worry about that extra point, boys," he said. "That guy happened to anticipate the kick and time his jump perfectly. But he's just one player out there, and as a team I know the Rangers are beatable. So let's go get 'em!"

The Clippers roared their determination and ran out of the locker room. This time, Terry joined the team that lined up on the field after the kickoff. He hunkered down in his usual spot. But then, remembering where the Rangers' nose tackle lined up, he inched forward as far as he could without being offside.

Then he raised his head just slightly and grimaced nastily at the Rangers' center. When play began, he flattened his opponent in a matter of moments and lunged after the quarterback. John Crum and Sid Keller seemed to have the same idea. Together, the three of them sacked the Rangers' quarterback.

Terry was amazed at how satisfied he felt.

The game against the Rangers ended in the Clippers' first victory of the season. The coach invited everyone to celebrate at the local pizza parlor. Many parents and friends decided to join in the festivities.

"It's better than cooking," said Mrs. McFee when she, Mr. McFee, and Nicky met Terry outside the locker room.

Nicky chattered about his running with the track team the whole way over to the restaurant. Terry tried to act interested, but he was barely listening. He was busy thinking about the game and the things he had learned by watching others play his position. About how the nose tackle had prevented the extra point.

When they got to the pizza parlor, Sid Keller called Terry over to join them. Terry wedged himself in with the other players. As he sat down he caught a glimpse of Nicky's disappointed face.

"Come on, Nicky," said Mrs. McFee. "We'll be right here in this booth next to theirs. Okay?"

Nicky slumped down beside her and stared at the tabletop. When his father asked what he wanted, Terry heard him mumble, "I don't care."

The pizza party lasted about an hour before people started getting ready to leave. Just before it broke up, Coach Butterfield thanked all the players for their hard work that day.

While he was speaking, Nicky drifted over to stand behind Terry.

"Everyone on the team played their best, and I'm really proud of you," the coach said. "I know you've heard it a million times, but, well, I'll say it once more: The Clippers can't be beat!"

"Go Clippers!"

"Rah team!"

"TER-REEE!"

Nicky's ear-splitting yell caught Terry completely

off guard. He whirled around and, before he could stop himself, said, "Nicky, pipe down! You're embarrassing me!"

Nicky didn't wait to hear any more. He ran back to the booth and cried, "I want to go home!"

11

Terry felt awful. He tried to apologize to Nicky the whole way home. But Nicky just leaned his head against the window and stared.

Mr. and Mrs. McFee did their best to get him to talk, too, but they had no better luck.

"Nothing to say," Nicky mumbled at one point.

They decided to leave him alone for the time being and hope he would come to them when he was ready.

But when he did, it wasn't to talk about Terry.

Nicky announced that he was through with track and wasn't interested in going out for the Special Olympics.

Terry didn't want to admit it, but he feared that Nicky's decision was his fault. He hadn't shown any interest in Nicky's progress with the track team for a long time. He hadn't paid much attention to him at the track during their morning exercises. But worst of all, he'd yelled at Nicky — yelled at him for shouting his encouragement and love for his older brother in front of his teammates and his parents.

Terry was so ashamed of himself he could barely look Nicky or his parents in the eye.

"I don't know what's happening between my two boys," Terry overheard Mr. McFee say to Mrs. Mc- Fee one night. "Used to be I couldn't find them around the house when I needed them. They'd be out horsing around in the yard or running at the track. Only place they seem to be now is holed up in their rooms."

Mrs. McFee murmured something that Terry couldn't hear.

"Well, I have an idea," Mr. McFee said. "Terry! Nicky! Come here, boys!"

Terry waited until he heard Nicky's door open, then walked into the kitchen. Nicky appeared moments later.

"How would you both like to join me out at the lake to bring back some firewood?" Mr. McFee asked them.

"I didn't know they were giving away firewood out there," said Mrs. McFee.

"The town cleared an area on the northern shore of the lake. All the hardwood trees in that area were cut into firewood lengths. It's first come, first served. I thought I'd load up the pickup and bring some back to use in the woodstove this winter," Mr. McFee explained. "And I sure could use some help."

Terry shrugged his shoulders. Why not? It *was* better than sitting around his room.

"Okay," he said. "When do you want to go?"

"Tomorrow morning," Mr. McFee said.

"Me, too," Nicky announced. "I'm going, too."

"Well, I'd love to join you, but there's only room for three in the truck," said Mrs. McFee.

"Plenty of room in the back," said Mr. McFee.

Mrs. McFee raised her eyebrows and looked over her glasses at him. "Any other bright ideas?" she asked sarcastically.

That brought a hoot of laughter from Terry. Even Nicky cracked a smile.

❁   ❁   ❁

The truck bumped up and down along the dirt road that wound its way through the woods. Outside, the birds were singing, and a light breeze rustled through the trees.

Inside the truck, all was silent. Mr. McFee had tried to start a conversation, but neither Terry nor Nicky responded with much enthusiasm. The night before, Terry had done everything he could think of to make up to Nicky. But Nicky had just looked at him with reproachful eyes. Finally, Terry had given up.

Mr. McFee slowed the truck as they came to the end of the road. On either side of them lay piles of logs, some big, some smaller.

"Okay, you two sourpusses," Mr. McFee said. "Why don't we load up the wood and then have lunch? If I remember correctly, we're not that far from the lake itself. We might even have lunch along the shore. Maybe by then you'll have thawed out enough to talk about whatever it is that's eating you."

Before leaving that morning, Mr. McFee had put together a surprise in the lunch basket. At the very bottom was all the makings for "s'mores" — graham crackers, chocolate bars, and marshmallows. If the sun stayed out and there was no wind, they could build a little fire and cook up their favorite outdoor dessert.

"Can we have lunch now?" asked Nicky.

"Not until we do some work," said Mr. McFee, pointing at a logpile. "And here it is. You guys ought to be able to handle some of those."

Terry walked over to the pile. "Here, Nicky, why don't you hold out your arms and let me pile a few logs on them? Then you can bring them over to the truck," Terry suggested.

"No, I don't need your help," Nicky said stubbornly. He bent over and started picking up logs until his arms were too full to hold any more. Then, one by one, the logs fell to the ground as Nicky desperately tried to hold them. Tears of frustration sprang into his eyes.

Terry was just about to see if he could help when Mr. McFee said briskly, "All right, let's get some organization going here. Terry, you climb into the back of the truck and stack the wood. That way we'll get a lot more in. Here, Nicky, let's try loading you up again, only maybe this time we'll give you just a couple of logs, okay? It'll be a lot easier and I'll bet you'll get more done that way. I'll get the rest."

With Mr. McFee's system, Nicky was able to move a good amount of wood, and he cheered up a bit. For a while, the three McFees moved along like a well-oiled machine. In no time at all, the truck was almost half full.

"I'm hungry," Nicky announced, dropping two small pieces of wood over the tailgate. "And I'm tired, too."

"I could practically set my watch by your stomach, Nicky," joked Mr. McFee. "I don't even have to look at it to know that it's just about noontime."

"You're not wearing your watch," Nicky pointed out.

"I always leave it in the glove compartment when I'm doing rough work. Don't want it to get broken. Anyhow, I'm hungry, too. What say we eat?"

For the first time that day, both Terry and Nicky smiled.

"Hop in, boys," Mr. McFee said. "I want to move the truck so there'll be room for somebody else to drive in to get wood."

He drove over toward the lakeshore and parked the truck in a shady spot.

As Nicky jumped out, he almost fell. The incline was steeper than it looked.

Terry hopped off the back and walked to the water's edge without a word. He was tired from all the work he had done, but he felt good standing in the warm sunshine. When he turned back toward the truck, he saw his father lugging a big cooler with both hands. Nicky was carrying a large thermos bottle.

"Here, let me help," he called over to them.

"No, we can do it," said Nicky.

"Why don't you gather some small pieces of wood for kindling? And some rocks. We'll have a small fire. It's a little cool when you stop working."

While Terry was foraging, Mr. McFee rolled over three large logs. He placed them around the spot he'd chosen for the fire. It was close to the water so that they could douse the flames quickly if the wind came up.

Once Terry returned with the wood, it didn't take long to get a nice fire going. Nicky looked disappointed when he discovered that they weren't going to be cooking hot dogs and hamburgers. But the "everything in the fridge" hero sandwiches made up for it. And no one complained when Mr. McFee dug into the bottom of the cooler and pulled up the fixings for s'mores.

"Oh, boy!" shouted Nicky. He looked happier than he had for hours.

Or was it days? Terry thought suddenly. I can't remember the last time Nicky looked that enthusiastic about anything.

He had an inspiration. "I'll race you to the best marshmallow skewer!" he cried. "Bet I can have one made before you!"

Nicky jumped to his feet and sprinted for the trees. "No, sir!" he called over his shoulder. He grabbed the first long twig he could find, raced back to the fire, stabbed a marshmallow, and stuck it in the flames. By the time Terry got back, both the twig and the marshmallow had fallen into the fire.

"Well, it smells good anyway," said Mr. McFee, laughing. "Take your time, Nicky. There's enough for seconds."

After they had their fill, Terry waited for Mr. McFee to start the serious talk he knew was coming. His father had all but promised to get to the heart of the matter after lunch, and he wasn't one to go back on his word.

But the sun came back out from behind the clouds and shone brightly on the grassy shore.

"I think I'll just catch forty winks," said Mr. Mc-Fee. He stretched out next to his log seat, pulled his cap over his eyes, and was snoring quietly in minutes.

Terry looked at Nicky. Now that they were alone, he felt awkward. He wanted to tell Nicky he was sorry for not having paid much attention to him and his running lately, and for having yelled at him in the pizza parlor the night before. Instead, he said, "Come on. We'll surprise him. Let's get this stuff back into the truck."

Nicky nodded. They cleared off the picnic blanket and shook it out down near the shore. Then the two of them piled up all the luncheon things and stuffed them into the cooler.

"Aren't we going to wash them?" Nicky asked.

"We can do a better job when we get home," Terry answered. He threw the empty soft drink cans into the cooler and closed the lid.

"All we have to do is put some water in those cans. We don't have to wash them with soap," Nicky said.

"Look, we can do it all when we get back," Terry insisted. "Let's just get this into the truck. You take the thermos."

"I can take the cooler," Nicky said.

"The thermos is lighter," said Terry somewhat irritably. "You can't handle the cooler."

"You don't know what I can do!" Nicky shouted.

"Shhh! You'll wake up Dad!" Terry said with a hiss. "Just take something and bring it over to the truck, will you?"

Nicky stubbornly dragged the cooler along the ground. Terry sighed and picked up the thermos.

He reached the truck before Nicky, climbed inside, and stowed the thermos behind the front seat. Then he turned around to help Nicky.

The younger boy started to climb in next to Terry. "I want to see what time it is," he said.

"That can wait," said Terry.

"Let me see Dad's watch!" cried Nicky. He reached toward the glove compartment.

"Just let me get the cooler in first." Terry tried to reach past him.

But Nicky wouldn't let him. "No, I can do it!" he said angrily. He clumsily swung the cooler onto the front seat. As he did, the lid flew off and sliced right at Terry's head.

"Watch it!" he cried, hurling himself back out of the way.

"Ouch!" he shouted as his back came into contact with something blunt and hard. He scrambled out of the truck.

"It didn't even hit you!" Nicky said, staring at him.

No, Terry knew it wasn't the cooler that hurt

him. He'd banged up against something inside the truck.

It might have been the parking brake. It might have been the gearshift. He didn't have a chance to find out, because whatever it was that had shaken loose didn't matter. What was really important right at that moment was that the truck was rolling down the slope — and heading right toward the lake!

12

Terry jumped up and started running toward the truck.

"DADDY!" Nicky screamed at the top of his lungs.

Mr. McFee leaped to his feet and shouted, "Get back! Both of you!"

As it reached the level ground at the bottom of the slope, the truck started to slow down. It looked to Terry as though it might not end up in the water after all.

Mr. McFee ran over in the direction of the moving vehicle. When it seemed as though it would be safe to grab hold of the door, he reached for the handle on the driver's side.

The danger of the truck rolling into the lake looked as though it was over.

But then something happened that surprised everyone. The truck hit a soft spot and started to sink down on one side. The door swung open and crashed into Mr. McFee. It hit him broadside on the head and knocked him backward.

For a minute, it even seemed like the truck might fall on top of him.

Then, suddenly, it stopped sinking.

Wide-eyed in amazement, the two boys dashed over to their father. He was lying on the ground and not moving.

Terry was speechless when he saw Mr. McFee sprawled out there.

"Is . . . is he . . . ?" Nicky asked, trembling.

Terry bent over and put his ear to Mr. McFee's chest.

"I can hear his heart beating," he said to Nicky. "And, look, see his chest move. He's breathing. Dad! Dad, wake up!"

"Come on, Dad! Open your eyes!" Nicky cried.

But Mr. McFee continued to lie there without a flicker of an eyelid.

"He's out cold," Terry announced.

"What'll we do?" Nicky asked. "What's going to happen?"

"I don't know," said Terry. "But we have to get him away from here. What if the truck starts to go over? It could fall right on top of him."

"Can we move him? He's so big," said the younger boy, still quivering.

"We have to do this carefully so we don't hurt him," said Terry. "Remember that class we all had to take in school? You know, about first aid?"

"I think so," said Nicky. "They said you have to cover up the person that's hurt."

"Good. Then you go get the picnic blanket while I get started," said Terry.

"You sure? Can't I help?" Nicky asked.

"Let me see what I can do," said Terry. "Just get the blanket."

Nicky ran off in search of the big square piece of cloth.

Kneeling down next to Mr. McFee, Terry slid his hands gently under his father's shoulders. Then, grabbing hold beneath his upper arms, he began to

136

drag Mr. McFee backward, away from the truck.

It was an awkward position. Terry could move only a few inches at a time — and it took all his strength to keep from jerking or falling over. But he knew he had to be careful. What if something were broken? One wrong move could make it worse.

It seemed like an hour had passed when he heard Nicky say, "Far enough. He's out of the way now." Indeed, they were close to the smoldering campfire, well off from the sinking truck.

"Good," said Terry, breathing heavily. The sweat was pouring down his face. He felt like he'd been slogging through a hot swamp. "Cover him with the blanket."

Nicky came up next to his father and spread the big checkerboard cloth over him.

"He's still out like a light," said Terry. "We have to get some help."

"Can you drive the truck?" Nicky asked.

"No way!" Terry replied. "Even if I knew how, look at it!"

"Dad could get it out," Nicky said.

"Well, I'm not Dad," said Terry. "No, we're not getting out on the truck. But we have to get help out here — and we have to do it fast."

"But . . . but we can't just leave Dad here," said Nicky. "What if some animals —?"

"We're not leaving him," said Terry. He looked Nicky right in the eye. "One of us has to stay with him, and one of us has to go and get help."

Nicky stared at his brother. Then he looked down at his father.

"I'll stay," he said to Terry. "You go."

"Nicky, don't be dumb," Terry said. "I'm better off staying with him. What if he starts to get up, or tries to move?"

"I could make him be quiet," said Nicky. "I'd tell him not to move."

"Listen, kiddo, we don't have a lot of time here," said Terry, quietly. "It's starting to get cloudy, and it might begin to rain. Then we'll be in a lot of trouble. If you leave now and run as fast as you ever have, you can get to the end of the road real soon. There should be someone in the booth at the park entrance who can help you."

"I can't," mumbled Nicky.

"What do you mean? Of course you can," said Terry.

"No, I can't! I can't!" Nicky shouted.

Terry took a deep breath. He wasn't even sure what he was going to say to convince Nicky until he'd suddenly blurted it out.

"Listen, Nicky, you're a born runner. I'm not half the runner you are. I think — I think that's part of the reason why I haven't gone running with you lately. And why I haven't helped you out with your running when I did. I guess I'm jealous of you. But I realize now that even if I'll never be a great runner again, I'm good at other things — like being strong enough to move Dad. And I'm tough enough to take care of him until you get back. But we don't have time to be talking about stuff like this! Plain and simple, you'll be able to get to help quicker than I will! Nicky, you've got to go now!"

"You promise to take care of Dad until I get back?" Nicky asked, wide-eyed.

"I promise," Terry said. "Now hit the road — and let's see you set a new world's record!"

139

Nicky nodded quickly. He bent over and kissed his father on the forehead.

Then he went for it. In a few seconds he was out of sight.

Terry took off his jacket and gently placed it on Mr. McFee. Then he grabbed some more wood and added it to the still burning fire. The flames soon rose up and cast a warm glow. Even if it got dark, they would probably be warm and safe. Better yet, the light would be a beacon for Nicky and the rescuers.

He settled down, cross-legged, next to Mr. Mc-Fee and stared at him. Now that Nicky was gone, Terry felt tired — and something else. As he started to shake, he realized that he, too, was scared. But he knew he had to tough it out until help came.

As the warmth of the fire crept over his back, he stop shaking and calmed down. Every few seconds he bent over Mr. McFee to make sure he was breathing. That was about all he could do.

Gradually the few seconds turned to minutes,

and Terry's eyelids began to flutter. Before he knew it, he slowly drifted off.

Everything grew dark. Then, one by one, shapes began to form in the distance. Through the dark, they looked like a football team coming downfield right at him. They grew bigger and ran faster and faster until they were almost on top of him.

But he wasn't afraid of them. He could stand his ground. He was bigger than they were and stronger than they were. And he knew just how to deal with them! After all, he was not only a tackle, but also a *fighting tackle* — the best there was!

At the same time, far off somewhere behind the dark shapes there was a loud crashing sound. As it grew louder, his eyes opened and he could see that it really had gotten darker.

His father! Mr. McFee was lying there on the ground in front of him, the same way he was when Terry last checked.

By now he knew that the noise was real, not a dream. It came from down the dirt road. As it got closer, he could see it was a dark black-and-white police car with the blue light on top flashing. And right behind there was an ambulance.

They pulled up right next to Mr. McFee. A policeman got out of his car, followed by Nicky, who jumped out the passenger door.

The EMTs went right to work, surrounding Mr. McFee so that Terry and Nicky couldn't see what was happening. But they could smell something strange and medicinelike in the air.

"Where am I? What happened? Who are you and —"

It was Mr. McFee talking!

Then one of the EMTs interrupted him. "Just stay calm and don't move," she said. "It looks like you're okay, but we have to check you out. You were struck on the head and you probably have a concussion."

Nicky called out, "Dad! It's me, Nicky!"

"And I'm here, too, Dad," Terry added.

They could hear the EMT saying, "The boys are just fine," as the medical team continued to do their work.

The policeman pulled the boys off to one side.

"Your father's a lucky man," he said. "It doesn't look as though he's badly hurt. But he might have been in trouble if we hadn't gotten here as soon as we did."

Terry pulled Nicky close to him. He was so proud of his little brother, he couldn't say a word.

One of the EMTs came over to them.

"Everything checks out here, but we're going to take him back to the hospital to make sure. You guys want to come along?"

"Go ahead," said the policeman. "I'll take care of everything here."

Before he finished speaking, the two McFee boys were at their father's side inside the ambulance.

"Dad, wait till you hear —"

"Dad, listen to this —"

Each of them could hardly wait to tell him what a great job the other one did. If Mr. McFee hadn't waved a finger at them to interrupt, they might have gone on for the entire trip back.

"Let me get one word in," he said softly. "I

just want to tell you I'm real proud of both of you."

A few weeks later, a delivery truck pulled up next to the McFee house. The driver took out two packages, a large one and a small one.

Mr. McFee answered the doorbell when it rang.

"Great," he said to the driver. "Just leave them on the porch. Thank you."

When the truck took off, he went back inside and called, "Terry! Nicky! Delivery for you!"

The two boys came rushing down the stairs.

"Delivery? What is it?" asked Terry. "Did Mom order some yucky new clothes from a catalog?"

"Is it my birthday present? It's not till next month," said Nicky.

Mr. McFee laughed. "Look at the two of you, so suspicious. Why don't you just go out on the porch and open your packages? Maybe they just came for you because someone thinks you ought to have a treat once in a while."

Torn tape and cardboard went flying as the packages were ripped open.

145

"Wow! Super running shoes," said Nicky. "Look, Terry, they've got all that stuff like on TV. Same as those guys wear in the Olympics!"

"They're for somebody who belongs right up there with the gold medal winners," said Mr. McFee.

"Boy, wait until my Special Olympics coach sees these," said Nicky. "I'm going to win every race!"

It took Terry a lot longer to open his package because there were so many pieces.

"My own workout bench, wow! Dad, you're going to have to help me assemble this," he said. "Hey, Nicky, look at these attachments. I'm going to be the strongest guy in that line."

"You're already number one in my lineup," said his father.

"Thanks, Dad," said Terry. "But I'm going to have to work hard to stay in the coach's starting lineup. And now, you'll see, I'm going to earn that job by being not only the biggest guy around, but the strongest and best as well."

"Okay, Atlas," said his father. "Let's see if we can figure out how to put this thing together."

"Me, too," said Nicky, stomping around in his new running shoes. "I want to help."

"Okay, you can help," said Terry. "And when we're through, I might just race you around the track. Just to make sure those new shoes are any good."

"You mean it?" asked Nicky. "You really want to run with me, like we used to?"

"Anytime, sport," said Terry. "Anytime."

How many of these Matt Christopher sports classics have you read?

- ❑ Baseball Flyhawk
- ❑ Baseball Pals
- ❑ The Basket Counts
- ❑ Catch That Pass!
- ❑ Catcher with a Glass Arm
- ❑ Challenge at Second Base
- ❑ The Comeback Challenge
- ❑ The Counterfeit Tackle
- ❑ Crackerjack Halfback
- ❑ The Diamond Champs
- ❑ Dirt Bike Racer
- ❑ Dirt Bike Runaway
- ❑ Face-Off
- ❑ Fighting Tackle
- ❑ Football Fugitive
- ❑ The Fox Steals Home
- ❑ The Great Quarterback Switch
- ❑ Hard Drive to Short
- ❑ The Hockey Machine
- ❑ Ice Magic
- ❑ Johnny Long Legs
- ❑ The Kid Who Only Hit Homers
- ❑ Little Lefty
- ❑ Long Shot for Paul
- ❑ Long Stretch at First Base
- ❑ Look Who's Playing First Base
- ❑ Miracle at the Plate
- ❑ No Arm in Left Field
- ❑ Olympic Dream
- ❑ Penalty Shot
- ❑ Pressure Play
- ❑ Red-Hot Hightops
- ❑ Return of the Home Run Kid
- ❑ Run, Billy, Run
- ❑ Shoot for the Hoop
- ❑ Shortstop from Tokyo
- ❑ Skateboard Tough
- ❑ Soccer Halfback
- ❑ The Submarine Pitch
- ❑ Supercharged Infield
- ❑ Tackle Without a Team
- ❑ Takedown
- ❑ Tight End
- ❑ Too Hot to Handle
- ❑ Top Wing
- ❑ Touchdown for Tommy
- ❑ Tough to Tackle
- ❑ Undercover Tailback
- ❑ Wingman on Ice
- ❑ The Winning Stroke
- ❑ The Year Mom Won the Pennant

All available in paperback from Little, Brown and Company